4/04=6
8/07= 11

DUEL
AT
GOLD BUTTES

DUEL
AT
GOLD BUTTES

Bill Pronzini and
Jeff Wallmann

G.K. Hall & Co. • **Chivers Press**
Waterville, Maine USA Bath, England

This Large Print edition is published by G.K. Hall & Co., USA
and by Chivers Press, England.

Published in 2001 in the U.S. by arrangement with Golden West
Literary Agency.

Published in 2002 in the U.K. by arrangement with Golden West
Literary Agency.

U.S. Hardcover 0-7838-9541-0 (Western Series Edition)
U.K. Hardcover 0-7540-4785-7 (Chivers Large Print)
U.K. Softcover 0-7540-4786-5 (Camden Large Print)

The text of this Large Print edition is unabridged.
Other aspects of the book may vary from the original edition.

Set in 16 pt. Plantin.

Printed in the United States on permanent paper.

British Library Cataloguing in Publication Data available

Library of Congress Cataloging-in-Publication Data

Pronzini, Bill.
  Duel at Gold Buttes / Bill Pronzini and Jeff Wallmann.
    p. cm.
  ISBN 0-7838-9541-0 (lg. print : hc : alk. paper)
  1. Large type books. I. Wallmann, Jeffrey M., 1941–
PS3566.R67 D84 2001
  813′.54—dc21   2001026380

DUEL
AT
GOLD BUTTES

One

It was just past noonday when Glencannon topped a bare limestone ridge and had his first look at the Dakotas settlement of Wild Horse.

He eased his sorrel into the shadow of an overhang and squinted down across miles of flat prairie land at the distant group of buildings. The shimmering heat haze made them look wavy and indistinct, like a mirage. But he could tell that Wild Horse was a pretty good-sized place, even for a railhead. The unbroken line of a Union Pacific spur cut through it from east to west, roughly paralleling the winding path of the Wild Horse River along which the town had been built. A mile to this side, the tracks hooked northwest across the flatlands and the river curled southeast into the labyrinth of gullies, carps, and rocky bluffs that formed the badlands section known as Gold Buttes.

Glencannon took off his hat and wiped his angular, sun-blackened face with a bandana. Hidden under his long black hair, the scar where his right ear should have been itched and burned, the way it always did in the heat. He rubbed it dry, retied the bandana, and then reached into his shirt pocket for the crumpled envelope, the kind that unfolds to become a letter. He knew from memory what the letter said, but he smiled again at the block lettering.

Jim,

We heard you are back in the Dakotas and working at Rowan's spread now. That's fine news. We have been hoping you would drift back to this part of the country some day.

Laurie and I are living near Wild Horse, about a two day ride from you. Can you come visit us after the fall roundup? Laurie says to expect to stay a week or more, as there is that much old times to chew over.

Your friend,
Clay Brewer

Below the note was a simple map showing where Brewer's ranch lay in relation to Wild Horse. Glencannon lifted his eyes from the letter and peered out at the town again. According to the map, the Brewers lived a good ten miles to the southeast, near Gold Buttes. A long ride, he thought. He'd been in the saddle since dawn, and both he and the sorrel were tired and sun-parched. Best to take a night's lodging in Wild Horse, he decided, and ride out to Clay's fresh in the morning.

He returned the letter to his pocket, then urged the horse out of the shade and down along the trail. As he rode, he thought about Laurie and Clay and how their pasts intertwined with his. . . .

Glencannon's parents, Scots from Pennsylvania, had been one of the first families to settle in the western section of Oklahoma after the Civil War. Although there hadn't been any major battles fought in the territory, there had been numerous skirmishes between the Unionists and the Confederacy; and the Choctaw, Cherokee, and Chickasaw Indian nations, among others, had signed treaties of alliance with the South. As punishment, the victorious North had driven these tribes from their lands and started assigning the property to homesteaders and ranchers. The Plains Indians hadn't taken kindly to this, rebelling and marauding for several years afterward.

In 1867, during one of their hit-and-run strikes, the Pawnees had massacred Glencannon's parents. He had been fifteen at the time. The only reason he had survived was that a Pawnee arrow had sliced off his ear, leaving him unconscious, and he had been mistaken for dead. As it was, he had nearly bled to death before help arrived.

Laurie's parents, the Overholts, had taken him in. They were Texans who, after driving their cattle from the Panhandle to the railroads in Kansas, had decided to relocate on Oklahoma's virgin grasslands, just as the Glencannons had done. But when the Indian situation steadily worsened in the year following the Glencannon massacre, and then an outbreak of anthrax had killed off most of their herd, the Overholts had decided to pull stakes again. This time, with Glencannon in tow, they had moved to the Dakotas and built a ranch near the Cheyenne River, east of Belle Fourche.

Laurie was a year younger than Glencannon, and they had become close friends. At times he'd felt she cared for him and might consent to be his wife, yet he'd never allowed himself to carry on with her. Part of the reason was a restlessness, a fiddlefooted need to see and do things before he settled down. And part of it was his missing ear. Despite Laurie's apparent unconcern with the deformity, he felt shamed and self-conscious about it, as if he were something less than a whole man. That was why he'd let his hair grow long and kept it that way — to hide his scar from curious and pitying eyes, particularly those of women like Laurie.

Well, Clay Brewer had been better for her, he had to admit that. Clay's father, old Tom Brewer, had come from Wyoming to open a mercantile store in a nearby Dakotas settlement, and after the night Clay and Laurie met at a social on her eighteenth birthday, there were no other men for her. Brewer had the dependable, responsible streak Glencannon lacked, was intelligent and a mule when it came to work, and everyone had agreed that he was a damn fine catch. Brewer had gone to work for Overholt to learn the business of ranching, and after a six-month courtship, had married Laurie.

Glencannon had stayed on with the Overholts until the christening of the Brewers' first-born, a son, Dale, and then began his wandering ways. He'd returned to the Dakotas a half-dozen times, to visit the Overholts and the Brewers, each time feeling a bittersweet pensiveness as he'd mark how Laurie was maturing, Dale was growing, Clay was industriously saving for a spread of his own. The rest of the time he'd drift from one spot to another throughout the West, working at anything from rail splitter to cattle drover. Now, a good decade and a half later, he was still circling the land, still unsure of what he wanted but knowing he hadn't as yet found it.

This past summer, he had counted himself lucky when he'd been hired as a hand by King Rowan. Rowan's huge spread in southeastern Dakota Territory was one of the finest around, noted for its high pay and square dealing. He'd hoped the job would last past the fall roundup — he preferred tending cattle, working the open range, to other ways of earning his forty-and-found — but it hadn't panned out that way. Along with several other seasonal hands, he'd been given his leave, with bonus, two days ago.

He didn't know what he would do next, once his visit with the Brewers at their new spread was finished. Keep on drifting, he supposed. Once a fiddlefoot, always a fiddlefoot. His whole life seemed destined to be one long trail, sometimes

11

dry, sometimes muddy, always lonely.

It was another hour before Glencannon reached Wild Horse. He passed through the railroad yard, where the scream of locomotive whistles, the smell of hot oil, and the bawling of penned cattle filled the hot afternoon air. When he reached Range Avenue, the main street, he saw that it was alive with activity. Because it was the end of the fall work season for cattlemen and farmers alike, and for the men who worked for them, pockets bulged and there was almost a carnival atmosphere in the town.

Glencannon walked his mount along the dusty street. Saloons flourished on three of the five blocks in the central district; these were called The Lucky Buck, Ace High, and The Gold Strike. There were two general stores, a church that would double as schoolhouse, a saddle shop, a bakery, a funeral parlor, a shoemaker's, a cafe, a combination sheriff's office and jail made of stone-and-mortar and sporting a shingle that said *Harrison Oldham, Sheriff*, and an imposing four-story hotel called The Mason House. A sign hanging above the hotel entrance proclaimed: *The Softest Beds West of Saint Louis.* Glencannon grinned and said to himself, "We'll see about that."

The livery stable was at the far end of Range Avenue, at Fifth Street not far from the River. When Glencannon reached it he reined in before the open doors and dismounted. It looked cool inside; the owner had been wise enough to have covered the roof with sod, which not only helped to keep out the heat but would insulate the stable against winter blizzards.

A wizened, grizzle-bearded old man came out, wiping gnarled hands on a leather blacksmith's apron. "Help you, mister?" he asked around a thick cud of blackstrap.

"How much to feed and bed my horse?"

"Just for the day?"

"Just that."

"Fifty cents," the old man said, and spat a thin stream of tobacco juice into the dust at his feet.

Glencannon raised an eyebrow. "Seems a mite high."

"Depends on how you look at it." The old man's watery eyes seemed to be challenging him to haggle over the price.

But Glencannon was too weary to stand arguing in the hot sun. He shrugged, paid the fifty cents, took his saddlebags, and then joined the flow of people on the plank sidewalks.

He stopped into one of the general stores and used some of the Rowan bonus to outfit himself in a new pair of Levi's and a new cotton shirt. Then he went to The Mason House. A clerk with a face as stiff as his celluloid collar gave Glencannon one of the last available rooms, for the outrageous price of two dollars, and assured him that there was a bath on each floor and fresh water in the tubs.

Glencannon relaxed in the one on his floor for almost an hour, soaking away trail dust and fatigue. Back in his room, he closed the window curtains and lay down on the bed. The Mason House hadn't exaggerated their boast of the Softest Beds West of Saint Louis; he was asleep within minutes.

He awoke near dusk, brought upright by the sound of a gunshot and yelling from the street. He went to the window, looked out. But it was only a drunken cowhand showing off. The growling in his belly said it was time to get something to eat. He dressed in his new clothes, put his saddlebags under the bed, and locked the door after him as he left.

There was no dining room in the hotel, but the clerk, who was reading a dime novel through scratched spectacles, suggested a place called the Elite Cafe on Fourth. The food there turned out to be tolerably good, and a damn sight better than the hardtack and beans Glencannon had been feeding himself the past two days.

Close by the Elite was the saloon called Ace High. Glencannon went in through the batwings. The place was jammed with early-evening revelers, most of them congregated around roulette and poker tables. He pushed through the crowd, found a place at the plank bar, and called out for a beer. The two perspiring bartenders were drawing suds as fast as they were able; a foaming glass came sliding down to him half a minute later.

Behind the plank, above rows of whiskey bottles and casks of cheap brandy, was a badly done oil painting of a half-nude woman on a velvet settee. The frame of the painting was of wide, stained wood, inlaid with thin strips of mirror; Glencannon watched the reflected activity behind him as he drank.

He had been there less than five minutes when the batwings burst open and a gangly tow-headed youth came running inside. "It's the Wagon!" he yelled above the din. "Hey, the Dollar Wagon's here!"

The youth's word had an immediate effect on the customers. Shouting and laughing, more than half of them began to shove toward the street.

Glencannon turned to one of the bartenders, who was wiping his sweating face with a bar towel. "What's this Dollar Wagon?" he asked.

"Jersey Jack Halacy's travelin' store," the bartender told him. "You might as well go have a look-see, mister. This place is liable to be dead for awhile. Happens every time Halacy and his boys come to Wild Horse."

Glencannon waited until most of the men had emptied out of the saloon. Then he finished the last of his beer and went to see what the commotion was all about.

Two

In the gathering darkness Glencannon could see that a good percentage of the townspeople were headed south on Range Avenue, toward a grassy clearing beyond the livery stable. Sitting in the middle of the clearing, he saw as he approached, was a large brilliantly painted wagon hitched to a dappled gray; at least a dozen lanterns illuminated it and the area around it. A garish wooden sign fastened to the wagon's canvas side read:

HALACY'S DOLLAR WAGON

Fine Wares   *Patent Medicines*

Games of Chance

A tall, smiling man in a brocade vest and a fancy black waistcoat was standing beside the gray, joking loudly with a group of cowhands. At the rear of the wagon, two other fancy-dressed men were busily setting up an array of goods on the broad tailgate and on several felt-covered barrels on the ground to one side. An expectant buzz of conversation rippled through the crowd.

Glencannon made his way toward the front of the wagon. As he did, the tall man climbed up onto its wooden seat and removed his black silver-banded hat. He spread his arms wide.

"Friends!" he shouted in a voice as deep and powerful as a preacher's. "Friends and neighbors, ladies and gentlemen, good people of Dakota Territory's fastest growing community!"

The crowd grew silent. When the tall man had all eyes focused on him he went on, "Jersey Jack Halacy at your service, with a wagon brimful of the finest assortment of specialty items in this part of the Territory. Yes, friends and neighbors, hundreds of hard-to-find wares — and every single one of them available to you for the unbelievable price of one dollar or less. Think of it, friends. *One dollar or less!*"

While Halacy kept on talking, pitching the ladies first, the other two fancy-dressed men began to circulate through the crowd, holding up a variety of goods. Shiny pots and pans and other hardware items. Needles, an item much in demand in the Dakotas because they broke or disappeared often. Glass jewels. Sachets. Yards of calico and gingham.

Then Halacy appealed to the men, offering everything from clasp knives and pocket watches to a patent medicine called Doctor Modora's Tapeworm Remedy. For some reason, the major ill that year seemed to be tapeworms. Lack of correct diet, overwork and general fatigue, any ailment real or imagined was said to be the fault of worms. Glencannon had a good idea that there was just enough laxative in the medicine to make buyers believe it was doing some good;

chiefly, though, Doctor Modora's Tapeworm Remedy would consist of alcohol and rainwater.

The crowd was buzzing again. Halacy's spiel had worked them into a fever. Some were eagerly exchanging coins and paper money for favored goods, while others milled around the tailgate to examine the rest of the selection. A smaller group had begun to gather off to one side, where a fourth fancy-dressed gent had appeared. That one held a fan of cards in his right hand.

From the wagon seat Halacy was saying now, "And for those among you with a little sporting blood, a friendly game of three-card monte is about to begin for your profit and pleasure. Just one more service, friends, of Jersey Jack Halacy's one and only Dollar Wagon."

The slick-haired dandy with the cards seated himself on a packing crate behind one of the felt-covered barrels. The small knot of men, most of them half-drunk, surrounded him. Glencannon edged closer to watch the play.

The dealer turned three cards face up on the barrel top — a four of clubs, a nine of spades, and a queen of diamonds. Then he handed the remaining cards to the tow-headed youth who had run into the Ace High earlier, standing nearby, and told him to count them. The youth did that and announced that there were forty-nine cards left in the deck. The dealer then instructed him to put those cards in his pocket.

Glencannon had seen three-card monte

18

played before, in places such as Abilene and Deadwood. It was a simple little game. The dealer would turn the three cards on the barrel face down, sliding them over and under and across the felt. Then he would defy the player against him to pick the queen. Depending on his individual fortune and gambling courage, the player would then wager an amount of money from one dollar upward; whatever the amount, the dealer would match it. If the player succeeded in picking the queen, if his eye was quicker than the dealer's shuffling hands, the money was his. If not, the dealer collected the bet.

The men clustered nearer as the first game began. Glencannon watched the tow-head wager a five-dollar gold piece as the dealer deftly shuffled the three cards. The gangly youth pondered for a moment, then turned the middle card face up. It was the queen. The crowd hooted its approval, and the dealer called out, "Everybody wins, gents, everybody wins!"

The youth lost a second hand, a third, and gave way to a succession of other eager players. No pot was larger than five dollars, nor did the dealer win more than half the time. But when he did, the amounts were always larger than when he lost. Glencannon wondered if the monte game was as honest as it should have been. The dealer seemed too quick with his hands, indicating that a card here and there was palmed down to replace the queen. He'd seen enough monte to stand clear of the game himself, for just that reason. He didn't take kindly to being cheated.

He was about to turn and head back to the Ace High for another beer when a new player appeared before the barrel. Glencannon peered at the man's face in the lantern light, then broke into a grin.

"Clay!" he called. "Clay Brewer!"

The man spun around, squinting. He was as tall as Glencannon, though heavier, with massive shoulders and chest. He still had the same boyish good looks and curly black hair, though he seemed to have put on several pounds since Glencannon had last seen him. He wore a tan shirt and Levi's, and on his hip there was an old Dragoon Colt.

"Well, I'll be — Jim!"

"Place your bet," the dealer intoned. "Or let the next lucky gent step up."

Brewer came over to Glencannon and grabbed his hand. His flushed face said he'd been celebrating along with the rest of Wild Horse. "By God, Jim, it's good to see you. When'd you come in?"

"Past noon. I figured to ride out to your place early tomorrow."

"Hell, it's a good thing I came into town this afternoon, then." Brewer glanced back at the monte table. "Come on. I'm gonna win us some drinking money."

Glencannon started to protest, but Brewer

was already on his way back to the game. He followed silently. Brewer managed to move right up to the front of the line and placed a pair of one dollar bets. But he picked the nine of spades instead of the queen both times.

His face grew redder. He put two dollars down for the next wager, and lost again. The circle of men laughed, urging him to bet another time. Glencannon felt uncomfortable, then uneasy as Brewer lost three more times in succession and finally took the remaining coins from his Levi's, jingling them in his palm as the dealer riffled the cards.

"Clay," Glencannon began; but Brewer had already made up his mind. He slapped the money down.

"Lay 'em out!" he snapped, and the dealer shrugged and flipped the cards into position. Brewer pointed to the card on the right. "This one. That's the queen for sure."

It was the nine of spades again.

"Well, goddamn it!"

Glencannon stepped up quickly and clapped him on the arm. "Come on, Clay," he said. "I'll buy that drink."

Brewer allowed himself to be led away. "Christ, Jim, I don't understand it. I know the queen was there. I just *know* it." He shook his head, then lapsed into a moody silence.

The Gold Strike was the first saloon they came to. Glencannon ordered a set-up from one of the bargirls, declined her invitation to join them.

21

"How're Laurie and Dale?" he asked Brewer, hoping to take his friend's mind off the monte game.

"Well enough, I reckon."

"Dale's what now — sixteen?"

"Come winter."

Glencannon took a sack of Bull Durham from his shirt pocket and built himself a shuck. "Laurie still as pretty as ever?"

Brewer nodded. But there was something clouded-up in his eyes that Glencannon couldn't read. "Still hot-tempered, too. Likely she'll set into me good when we get home."

"How so?"

"That money I just lost at monte," Brewer said. "It was to be put aside so's she could outfit us for the winter. We ain't had much the past couple of years . . ." His voice trailed off into silence.

The bargirl brought a bottle of rye and two glasses. If the Brewers had been having a run of hard luck, Glencannon thought as he poured, why had Clay got into the game at all? He'd never been much of a gambling man, nor had he been foolish where money was concerned.

Glencannon dragged on his cigarette and said, "I remember as how you figured to do pretty well in this part of the Territory. What happened?"

Brewer shrugged. He put away his rye and refilled the glass. "Land I wanted was' sold between the time I first saw it and I got together enough money; I had to settle for a lesser parcel. Cattle got sick the first year and I lost most of the herd — over a hundred head. Turned out to be bad water and another well had to be dug."

"Rough."

Brewer drank again. "Then, last fall, Laurie came up in a family way."

"You finally had another youngster? Say, that's fine news!"

Brewer seemed not to hear him. A dark, pained expression came into his eyes. "Little girl, it was," he said in a monotone, "born in the dead of winter last. Looked just like Laurie. But there was something wrong with her; she couldn't seem to take her breath. By the time I could fetch a doctor, she was gone."

Glencannon could have bitten his tongue. He knew how much Clay and Laurie had wanted another child. He said, "Hell, Clay, I'm sorry . . ."

"Nothing for you to be sorry about."

Studying him, Glencannon realized that Clay Brewer had changed a good deal since they'd last met. He'd never been a man to allow bad luck or tragedy to pull him down; he had always been the strong shoulder, the encouraging voice, for others beset by hard times. Now, it was as if he'd somehow lost his zest for life.

"Damn rotten luck," Brewer muttered, his eyes brooding on the rye bottle. "Likely I'd have lost that monte if the cards had been face up."

"Maybe so," Glencannon said. He was still

thinking about the change in Brewer.

"How's that?"

"Sometimes monte is doctored, that's all."

"Hell! You mean Halacy's game is crooked?"

"Easy now, I'm not making any accusations. I'm only saying monte can be doctored."

Brewer leaned across the table. "How?"

"Palming the queen and replacing it with another card."

"No chance. I watched that dealer pretty close."

"Sure you did," Glencannon said. He didn't like the sudden anger that had begun to burn in his friend's eyes, and for the second time he felt like biting his tongue. "Reckon the game's all right, then."

"But he was pretty damned fast with his hands, at that," Brewer said slowly. "Funny how I kept getting that spade nine every time. Hell! Doctored — sure it was!"

"Simmer down, Clay —"

But Brewer was on his feet. "I'm goin' back to that wagon, Jim! I'm goin' back there and get my money if I have to bust things up to do it!"

He wheeled and started for the batwings, his boots making sharp thuds on the wooden floor. Glencannon kicked back his chair, cursing himself for not having kept his mouth shut, and took after him. He caught up with Brewer on the street outside, put a hard hand on his shoulder.

"Let me be, Jim. I'm not gonna set still for being cheated. There ain't nobody alive who can

24

cheat Clay Brewer and get away with it."

"That's liquor talking. Cool off now, before you —"

Brewer threw off Glencannon's hand and pushed his way toward the clearing where the Dollar Wagon was, his head down and his big hands curled into fists at his sides. Glencannon, going after him again, was jostled by the crowd still packed around the wagon. He couldn't stop Brewer before his friend reached the dealer at the monte barrel.

"This game's crooked!" Brewer yelled. He was swaying slightly now, his face shining blood-dark in the lantern light. "Everybody hear what I'm sayin'? Jersey Jack Halacy's Dollar Wagon runs cooked monte!"

The crowd gentled down into silence. Not so much because they believed Brewer's words as because they sensed the outbreak of trouble. All eyes went to Clay Brewer, and to Glencannon as he finally reached Brewer's side.

"Clay, you damned fool —" Glencannon started, but the dealer had got to his feet and was standing with his legs spread wide, glaring at Brewer.

"You're a liar, mister."

"And I say you're a cheap grifter!" Brewer reached across the barrel and clutched the dealer by the lapels of his fancy coat. "I want my money back!"

The dealer's face twisted into a grimace. He brought his arms up as though to break the grip, then threw a short vicious punch that connected with Brewer's jaw, and sent him stumbling backward into the crowd. As the cowhands and ranchers scuttled away into a widening circle the dealer rushed around the barrel, his lips skinned back, and lifted a heavy boot toward Brewer's head.

Glencannon was already moving by then. He swung himself in front of the dealer, threw a hard left just above the man's ribcage that stopped him and straightened him up as if he'd run into a wall. But the dealer didn't go down right away. He grunted in surprise and pain and half-turned toward Glencannon, a glazed expression on his face like that of a stunned animal. The pupils of his eyes seemed to rattle from side to side as they sought to focus on his new assailant.

Then he grunted again, this time in rage, and swung a wild and clumsy right. Glencannon ducked under it, hammered another blow to the dealer's midsection, following it with a looping left cross that cracked off a cheekbone. Air belched out of the man's mouth; his head snapped back and his body twisted half around. Then his legs gave way and he fell sideways, straight and rigid like an axed tree. Dust spumed up around him when his body hit the ground.

Glencannon stood over him for a second, feeling the aftershock of the blows tingling in both arms. The dealer showed no signs of wanting to get up. Glencannon started to relax, turned his head to look for Brewer.

"Look out!" someone in the crowd shouted. "Behind you!"

Glencannon whirled, crouching, just in time to see one of the black-coated men from the Dollar Wagon closing in on him with a thick ash chair leg held high over his head. He tried to ward off the slashing blow that came in the next second, but he hadn't been able to set himself properly. The chair leg glanced off his arm, numbing it, and then glanced hard off the side of his head.

It felt as if a horse had kicked him in both places. He staggered, jarred down on his right hip. There was a wild ringing sensation in his ears; his vision blurred and the faces around him seemed to swim together in a dreamlike confusion of light and shadow.

He rolled over and dragged himself onto all fours. But he didn't seem to have enough strength to get up. He shook his head, kneeling there, and kept on shaking it until the ringing faded and the carousel behind his eyes slowed down and let him see again. Then he pushed up onto one knee, with the other foot planted flat on the ground.

"Hold it right there, son," a sharp voice commanded. "Fight's all over now. No more ruckus tonight."

Glencannon blinked and focused on the owner of the voice standing in front of him. The

27

man was short and thick through the middle, with long gray hair and a bushy, light-colored mustache that framed his mouth and hung limply over his chin. He was somewhere in his fifties and each decade of his life looked to be etched on the leather surface of his face. Pinned to the left hand pocket of his vest was a five-pointed star, and held in his right hand, gleaming where it caught the lantern glow, was a Colt .44.

Glencannon's head cleared enough for him to remember the shingle he'd seen on the jail building earlier: Harrison Oldham, Sheriff. He blew out a heavy breath, wincing, and let the tension ease out of him.

"That's right, son. Now you just get up nice and slow and come along with me. I reckon a night in jail'll cool you down some."

"Jail? Now wait a minute, sheriff —"

"Hell, Harrison," somebody in the crowd said, "this fella didn't start the trouble. It was Clay Brewer done that."

"Then Clay'll spend the night in jail too," Oldham said. "Along with this gent and the two from the Dollar Wagon. You know the town rules about disturbin' the peace and public brawling. Everybody involved gets arrested. No exceptions."

Glencannon, on his feet now, clutching his still-numb arm, searched the surrounding faces. Then his mouth quirked and he felt a mixture of disappointment and bitterness. Maybe everybody involved wasn't going to get arrested, after all, he thought. At least not right away.

Clay Brewer had disappeared.

Three

A thin shaft of sunlight slanting across his face woke him the next morning.

That, and the flies.

He could feel them walking on his face and hands, could hear them buzzing in his ears; his hands flailed reflexively to brush them away. Then he groaned, rolled onto his back, and opened his eyes. His head ached where the Dollar Wagon dandy had clubbed him. When he reached up a hand and touched the area above his missing right ear, he found it bruised and the skin broken. If it hadn't been for the thick mat of his hair, he thought, he might have considerably worse than a headache right now. He took his hand down, saw flakes of dried blood on the fingers, and grimaced. Now he knew what had attracted the damned flies.

Slowly, he eased himself to a sitting position on the hard wooden bunk. The jail cell was small, no more than a dozen feet square. The ceiling was made of gray rock, ringed with exposed wooden studs, the walls were bare stone-and-mortar, and the floor was made of worn planks stained almost black. In the outer wall was a high, small window crosshatched with heavy bars; the rust on them had been washed by the rains down the inner wall, staining the stone a dull ochre color. And in the wall facing the window was a thick timber door banded together with rusted iron straps, with a small eyehole cut in its center. The cell contained nothing except the bunk and a toilet bucket that gave off foul odors and was rimmed with flies.

Looking around him, Glencannon felt a fresh surge of anger. His first night in Wild Horse, and instead of spending it in the soft bed at The Mason House, he'd wound up in jail for no good reason except that he'd tried to help a friend. And what about Clay Brewer? Why had he run off as he had, leaving Glencannon to face the sheriff alone? Oldham hadn't found him, either, or at least he hadn't up until the time Glencannon dropped off into a painful sleep. And as if that wasn't enough, the two Dollar Wagon men the sheriff had arrested had been out of their cells and gone within a half-hour; Glencannon had heard them being released, the sound of their voices, the sound of Oldham's laughter and that of Jersey Jack Halacy.

Glencannon got to his feet, flexing his right arm. The soreness was gone from it, at least, except for a bruise that was tender to the touch. He moved across to the window, raised up to look out through the bars. He couldn't see much except bright sky and the swollen eye of the sun, half-open on the eastern horizon, visible beyond an alleyway between two buildings. Not long after sunrise, he thought. He kept on standing there, looking out and brooding about Clay Brewer.

He'd been doing that for five minutes or so when a deep voice bellowed, "Rise 'em!" from outside in the corridor. "Everybody up, now!"

Glencannon heard muffled retorts from the cells on either side of his. The brusque voice seemed to come closer, and the shouts of "Rise 'em!" were punctuated by the sounds of boot-falls and sharp raps against wood. Then a heavy fist landed on the door of his cell. When he heard the outside crossbar slide away he went over there, stood waiting as the door squeaked open.

Sheriff Oldham stood on the other side of it. He gave Glencannon a wry smile and said, "Morning, son. You don't look quite as feisty as you did last night."

"I wasn't feisty then. I told you what happened."

"Sure you did."

"You still think I was drunk, is that it?"

"Had liquor on your breath," Oldham said.

"I'd had a few drinks, yes, but I was sober."

"Don't matter much. Fact is, Glencannon, you were in a brawl and makin' a public nuisance of yourself, drunk *or* sober."

"How do you know my name?"

"Looked through your belongings last night. Part of my duty. I like to know who I got locked up in my jail."

"What about Clay Brewer?" Glencannon

asked. "Have you got *him* locked up in your jail?"

"Nope. Never did find him last night. But he'll pay for his part sooner or later, same as you."

Glencannon touched the sore spot above his missing ear. "You going to let me out of here now?"

"Well . . . maybe not just yet."

"When, then."

"Depends. If I've a mind to I could keep you locked up until the circuit judge rides through."

Glencannon scowled.

"That's two weeks, maybe three," Oldham said.

"You can't keep me in here that long! Listen, you let those two from the Dollar Wagon go a half-hour after you brought them in —"

"That's because Jersey Jack Halacy paid their fine."

"Fine?"

"Yep. As sheriff I'm empowered to collect fines for disturbin' the peace and other misdemeanors." His smile turned wolfish. "Saves the circuit judge considerable trouble. Besides, it don't hardly seem fair to jug a man for two, three weeks just so he can either pay the same fine or spend another thirty days in a cell."

"How much is the fine?"

"Twenty dollars."

"That's a lot of money."

Oldham shrugged, smoothing the ends of his drooping mustache with his fingertips. "Two, three weeks is a lot of time."

"Yeah." Glencannon held his temper, let out a breath between his teeth. "All right, sheriff. I'll pay the fine."

"Well, I'm glad to hear that. It's the smart way to go, son."

Glencannon didn't say anything. The sheriff beckoned him out of the cell, then followed him along the narrow corridor toward the open door at the far end, past two more cell doors behind which male voices grumbled. Oldham's office contained a scarred wooden desk, a swivel chair, a rifle cabinet with a pair of Winchester .70s inside it, and a sooty-looking potbellied stove. The front window was coated with enough dust to blur Glencannon's view of the street outside.

His personal effects, including cartridge belt and his Colt Peacemaker, were in a lower drawer of the desk. Oldham took them out, laid them on a stack of yellowed Wanted bulletins. "Check it over, son. Make sure nothing's missin'."

Glencannon took inventory, noting wryly when he opened his wallet that he had just twenty dollars in folding money. He thought that it was a good thing he'd left the rest of his money in his saddlebags at The Mason House; otherwise, his fine for disturbing the peace might have been higher.

"All there?" Oldham asked when he was done. Glencannon nodded and handed over the twenty dollars. Then he began to build himself a cigarette from his makings. "Mind if I ask you something, sheriff?"

"Go right ahead."

"You ever consider the possibility that monte game of Halacy's is crooked?"

Oldham studied him for a moment. "I considered it."

"And?"

"Well, in the first place, Halacy and his Dollar Wagon been comin' to Wild Horse regular two, three times a year for the past three, and most of the time they ain't no trouble at all. Just when some fellas get liquored up, like you and Clay Brewer done. And in the second place, I ain't seen no proof of illegal goings-on. Besides, the Wagon's good for Wild Horse business. Folks come from a ways out when Halacy and his boys are due."

"So you just look the other way while they're here."

"You're wrong about that, son," Oldham said, settling into the swivel chair behind his desk. "I keep an eye on Halacy, just like I keep an eye on everyone comes into Wild Horse."

Glencannon scratched a sulfur match and fired his cigarette. His anger at the sheriff and the man's ways still simmered, but it had no outlet; he couldn't afford to make any more trouble for himself. And he had to admit, reluctantly, that Oldham was no worse than most lawmen he'd encountered in his travels. It was a harsh, rugged, desolate land; law and order were almost always handled on a community basis, and justice was dispensed quickly, if often blindly. Oldham would have been hired for his ability to keep the peace, not for his formal law ability or sense of fair play. His salary would be dependent upon a strong image and sly wits, with whatever shady practices he indulged in being overlooked by the local citizens.

"Am I free to go now?" Glencannon asked him.

"Sure thing, son. A word to the wise, though. I'd keep away from Halacy and his Dollar Wagon, if I was you. Any more trouble, and you'll be my guest until the circuit judge comes through. I believe in givin' a man a second chance, but if he don't take advantage of it then I don't show him a third. Clear?"

"Clear enough."

"Good. Now I expect Clay Brewer rode on out to that tin-pot ranch of his last night. If you're a friend of his like you say, and you look him up, you tell him to shag his ass in here to see me in the next day or two. If he don't I'll come lookin' for him, and we both don't want that to happen."

"I'll tell him," Glencannon said, and pivoted on his heel and stomped out of the office.

Range Avenue was quiet, as if still sleeping off the effects of last night's merrymaking. A few shopkeepers were unshuttering their businesses and arranging displays, a couple of riders sagged lethargically in their saddles on the way out of town, a bleary cowhand was stumbling toward a nearby cafe for coffee. Otherwise, both the street and the sidewalks were empty.

As Glencannon strode along the boardwalk toward The Mason House, he thought again about Clay Brewer. The sheriff was probably right that Brewer had lit out for home after the Dollar Wagon brawl, drunk as he'd been. But the question was why? The Clay Brewer Glencannon had known in the past wouldn't have run away from trouble; he'd have stayed to see it through, and taken whatever the consequences were. There wasn't much doubt that Brewer was a changed man — changed for the worse. Glencannon vowed that he was going to find out what had done it, from Laurie if not from Clay himself.

When he reached The Mason House he asked the desk clerk if anyone had left a message for him, thinking that Brewer might have bothered before leaving town. But there were no messages. Upstairs, Glencannon found his chaps and saddlebags just as he had left them under the iron-frame bed. His head still throbbed, sending shoots of pain across the top of his skull. He poured water from a pitcher into a china basin, both of which had been set out on a sideboard, and gingerly washed away the dried blood above his temple. The gash there was three inches long, and the area around it was discolored and soft to the touch. It would need some tending to, he thought.

The smell of the filthy jail cell was on his

clothes; he changed back into his dusty trail outfit and left the new shirt and Levi's for the hotel laundry. Then he peeled off a few bills from his roll, put them into his wallet. Downstairs again, he turned in his key and got the address of one of Wild Horse's two doctors from the desk clerk.

The doctor charged him fifty cents to clean and bandage the scalp wound. Another fifty cents bought him a breakfast of steak and eggs at the Elite Cafe, just down the block. It was past nine o'clock when he came back out on Range Avenue, and the street was beginning to come alive with morning arrivals in buckboards and wagons. Over in the rail yards, the hoot of a locomotive's whistle rose through the gathering heat. The prospect of a long ride under a fiery sun didn't hold much appeal, particularly with his head still throbbing as it was. But it had to be done. He needed to talk to Brewer, and to carry the sheriff's warning to him; and he also wanted to pay his respects to Laurie and Dale.

He headed toward the livery stable. As he neared it he saw that the Dollar Wagon was no longer in the wide clearing beyond. Pulled up and gone already? he wondered. He went inside the stable, found the same wizened old man forking hay into one of the stalls, and called for his sorrel. While he helped the hostler with the saddle, Glencannon asked him, "What happened to Halacy's Wagon? Leave town, did they?"

"Nope, not yet." The hostler chewed ponderously on his everpresent blackstrap. "You can figure on them boys to puttin' on their hijinks for another day or two."

"Where do they camp?"

"Down by the river, usually. On Willow Flat."

"Where's that?"

"About a quarter-mile southeast of here," the old man said. He spat a dark, thick stream and squinted up at Glencannon. "If you're figurin' to look 'em up out there, I'd advise against it. Those boys like their privacy, if you catch my drift."

"I'm not sure I do."

"They already got enough company from town."

"Company?"

"Hell, boy, do I have to spell it out for you?" The old man spat again and then cackled without mirth. "Women. Painted women from The Gold Strike saloon. Now you understand?"

Glencannon nodded. He finished cinching the saddle before he spoke again. "Tell me, oldtimer — do you know Clay Brewer?"

"Got a ranch about ten miles from here? Sure, I know him."

"Does he usually put his horse up here when he comes to town?"

"Sometimes."

"How about yesterday?"

"Yep."

"Did he call for it last night while you were here?"

"Nope. Didn't call for it at all."

"You mean his horse is still here?"

The hostler shook his head. "Don't mean that. Somebody else called for it this morning, just past sun-up."

"Who?" Glencannon asked, frowning.

"Tow-headed kid, name of Barber. Said he was a friend of Brewer's and Brewer asked him to fetch the horse."

"Why couldn't Brewer fetch it himself?"

"Kid didn't say."

"Why'd you let him have the horse?"

"Why not? I seen him around Wild Horse before, mostly when the Dollar Wagon's in town. Besides, he paid me extra; said it was what Brewer wanted."

Glencannon began to feel a little uneasy. He did some ruminating, and remembered how the tow-head, Barber, had come running into the Ace High to announce the arrival of the Dollar Wagon; how the kid had been first up to the monte barrel, and how he'd won when most everyone else had lost. A shill who worked for Jersey Jack Halacy? That seemed a good bet. But the rest of it didn't make much sense, unless there was some kind of mischief involved. Why would Brewer send the tow-head to fetch his horse? Where had Clay spent the night, if not out at his ranch? And where was he now?

"You happen to see which direction the kid

took Brewer's horse?" Glencannon asked the hostler.

"Nope. Didn't pay attention. Why?"

Glencannon swung into leather. "Just curious, is all."

"I'd advise against that, too," the hostler said irascibly, and turned away to his chores.

Glencannon cantered the sorrel past the clearing to Placer Street, which looped around and became a wagon road leading out of Wild Horse along the river. He turned there, his lips pursed into a thin line, and headed southeast toward Willow Flat.

Four

When Glencannon came in sight of Willow Flat he saw that it was just that — a flat section of grassland, strewn with willow trees, at the edge of the sloping riverbank. The summer drought had turned the river into a slender murky stream; here, it was half-hidden beneath the cracked-earth wall of the bank. The Dollar Wagon sat in the middle of the flat, in the shade of a pair of willows. Off to one side, the dappled gray and three saddle horses were picketed and grazing. On the other side, nearest the river, were a pair of wedge-tents, two bedrolls, and a fire burning inside a ring of stones. The smell of woodsmoke was pungent in the hot morning air.

Three men were grouped around the fire, drinking coffee from tin cups. But when they saw Glencannon turn in off the road, all three of them got to their feet and stood stiffly, poised and watchful. Jersey Jack Halacy wasn't among them. Neither was the tow-headed kid, Barber. From inside one of the tents Glencannon could hear the sounds of a man's laughter and a woman's voice punctuated by giggles.

He drew rein and sat the sorrel in the same poised way the three men were standing, his left hand on the pommel and his right laid along his thigh, close to the Colt Peacemaker. Nobody said anything for a dozen seconds. Then one of the men — the slick-haired monte dealer Glencannon had beaten down during the brawl — stepped forward. His face was set in a cold, hard mask, but his eyes glowed bright and hot with suppressed fury.

"What the hell do you want here, mister?"

"I'm looking for a friend of mine," Glencannon said.

"You won't find any friends here."

"His name is Clay Brewer. He's the gent who accused you of cheating at monte last night."

The dealer's eyes seemed to spark. "That why you've come, is it? To make the same accusation?"

Inside the tent the laughter and giggling stopped abruptly. But Glencannon didn't look over there; he kept his gaze steady on the monte dealer's face. "You seen Clay Brewer since last night?" he asked in level tones.

"I asked *you* a question, mister."

"Answer mine and I'll answer yours."

"Listen, you —"

"Cool down, Jess," a voice said from the wedge-tent. Glencannon glanced in that direction, and saw that Jersey Jack Halacy had come out and was buttoning a ruffled white shirt over a pair of gray-striped britches. "No cause to get excited. Man's got a right to go looking for a friend."

The dealer, Jess, held Glencannon's eyes for a

moment. Then, reluctantly, he said, "I reckon that's so," and backed up to where the other two were. But his eyes kept on smouldering like the fire inside the ring of stones.

Halacy finished buttoning his shirt and moved over to stand between Glencannon and his three henchmen. He had thick black hair, worn long to the shoulders, and a lean, predatory face. His eyes were dark brown, almost black; they neither blinked much nor gave away anything of what was going on in the mind behind them. He reminded Glencannon of a hawk — calm, patient, deadly.

But for all that, his smile was easy and disarming. He used it now as he said, "You say your friend's name is Clay Brewer?"

"That's right."

"And your name?"

"Jim Glencannon. Have you seen Brewer since the fight last night?"

"I'm afraid not, Mr. Glencannon."

"So he didn't make a second pitch to get back the money he'd lost at monte."

"No."

"And if he had?"

"Why, I'd have referred him to Sheriff Oldham." Halacy spread his hands and shrugged. "Just as I'd do to you, Mr. Glencannon, if you were to accuse us of illegal gambling practices. The fact is, I run a perfectly honest monte game — nothing more than a service to my customers. We have nothing to hide."

Smooth, Glencannon thought. Silk-smooth. But you wouldn't want to turn your back on him if he had a gun and you didn't. "All right," he said, "you don't know where Brewer is. How about a tow-headed kid named Barber? You know him?"

No reaction. "Barber," Halacy said musingly. "No, I don't place the name. Is he another friend of yours?"

"I thought he might be a friend of *yours.*"

Halacy shook his head. Then he turned and said to the other three, "Any of you know this Barber gent? You, Luke?"

"Nope."

"Me neither," the dealer, Jess, said. "How come he's askin'?"

"Well, Mr. Glencannon?"

"As long as you don't know, it doesn't matter."

Another shrug. "Is there anything else we can do for you?" Halacy asked. "If not I have some, ah, unfinished business to attend to." He glanced over at the wedge-tent, then gave Glencannon a rakish wink. "I'm sure you understand."

"I understand, all right," Glencannon said. He also understood that there was no point in trying to press for more information. None of these men was going to admit anything, not with Halacy in charge; and with the odds at four to one, he'd be a fool to make any kind of trouble. "I'll be going, then. But I expect I'll see you again, Halacy."

"That's up to you," the other said, but the tone of his voice made it plain that it wouldn't be a good idea.

Glencannon gigged his horse around and started back toward the wagon road, riding at an angle so that he could watch the four men. None of them moved except for Halacy, who raised one hand in a mock salute and then pivoted toward the wedge-tent. The sudden giggling cry of a woman floated up again across the flat.

When he reached the road Glencannon turned south. According to the map Clay Brewer had drawn on the bottom of his letter, the Brewer ranch lay in that direction, not far from the badlands section called Gold Buttes. It was almost noon now, and overhead the sun was like a molten ingot in the cloudless sky. Glencannon rode slackly, shoulders slumped and shirt sweat-slicked, now and then keening the terrain with his eyes. But nothing moved in the shimmering heat except a pair of dark specks — hawks, maybe, or buzzards — some distance ahead along the river.

The sense of uneasiness rode with him. Maybe Brewer was all right and would be waiting when Glencannon reached the ranch; and yet what the hostler had told him about the tow-headed kid and Clay's horse, and the kind of hard cases Jersey Jack Halacy and his Dollar Wagon boys obviously were, made for a bad omen. What if Brewer had hidden somewhere last night, maybe with another bottle of rye, and then come around to the Dollar Wagon again to confront Halacy and the monte dealer? He'd been liquored up enough and angry enough to pull a fool stunt like that. What if he'd started waving his handgun around, demanding his money back, and what if — ?

Glencannon shook his head. Hell, he told himself, don't go jumping to conclusions. Take things as they come.

After a half-mile or so, he came to a fork in the road. The left fork, following the river, wasn't much more than a rock-strewn cow-trail. The right fork appeared to be a continuation of the wagon road and cut away due south, toward a round butte that rose above the heat haze like the crown of a tall bowler hat. Glencannon ran his tongue over parched lips, took Brewer's crumpled letter from his shirt pocket and studied the map. The right fork was the one he wanted, all right.

But he didn't turn along there. Instead he sat the sorrel and stared along the left fork to where it disappeared into a dark line of willow and cottonwood trees that greened the riverbank. Above the trees was what had caught his attention: three wheeling birds now, hard black and mottled red against the bright blue backdrop of the sky. Not hawks — buzzards. And that many buzzards in one place meant carrion of some kind, maybe a dead animal.

Or a dead man.

The uneasiness in Glencannon grew until it

was like a shrill, nervous wind. He kicked the sorrel to the left, along the rocky trail. A hundred rods along, the trail hooked left to follow a bend in the river and cut through the first stand of trees. They grew thick here and their branches cut off some of the fierce glare of the sun; but Glencannon scarcely noticed. He was still watching the irregular circling flight of the buzzards not far ahead.

He was just coming on another bend in the road, this one back to the right, when a horse nickered softly close by, hidden by trees and undergrowth beyond the bend. He drew sharp rein, his right hand dropping to the butt of the Colt Peacemaker at his side. The horse nickered again, then was still. There were no other sounds except for the droning of insects and the distant cries of the buzzards.

Glencannon gigged the sorrel, walked it into the bend. When he came halfway through it he could see a small grassy clearing that sloped down to the river's edge. The horse, a lean steel-dust, was tied to a bush a dozen rods off the trail. And down near the river, a single man sat with his knees drawn up, his arms folded on top of them and his head resting on his arms — asleep, maybe, or just resting. He wore no hat, and even at an angle part of his face was visible.

It was the tow-headed kid, Barber.

Glencannon dismounted. Saddle leather creaked as he did so, and the kid's head snapped up and around. Then he scrambled to his feet, awkwardly, grimacing as if he were in some kind of pain. A cartridge belt was slung around his waist, and the butt of an old single-action revolver showed in the single holster; the kid's hand hovered near it but didn't quite touch it. His expression showed fear, and something else that might have been guilt, as though he'd been caught doing wrong.

"Who are you?" he demanded in a quavering voice.

"Name's Glencannon. Yours'd be Barber, that right?"

The kid's eyes widened. "How'd you know that?"

"Hostler back in Wild Horse told me." Glencannon took a couple of steps forward, warily, his eyes moving from the kid's face down to his gunhand and back again. He kept his own hand, palm flat, on the holstered Peacemaker. "He also told me you called for Clay Brewer's horse this morning."

Barber swallowed three times in rapid succession, ran shaky fingers over his mouth and chin. Glencannon was close enough now to see that the kid had been in a fight of some sort; he had a purpling bruise under his right eye, one corner of his upper lip was split, and there were spots of blood on the front of his gray shirt. The shirt-cloth was also studded with a dozen or so burrs and grasstails, as if he'd been rolling around in — or maybe floundering through — heavy underbrush.

"About Clay Brewer's horse," Glencannon said.

"What about it?"

"Did you turn it over to him?"

"I . . . yeah, sure I did."

"Where?"

"In town. Over at the rail yards."

"What was Brewer doing there?"

"I dunno. I went over there looking for work and he come up to me and says I'll give you a dollar gold piece you go fetch my horse from the livery. So I done it and he rode off. That's all there is to it."

The hell that's all there is to it, Glencannon thought. It sounded like a rehearsed speech, rattled off from memory. He watched the kid through slitted eyes, not saying anything, until Barber began to fidget under his stare. The towhead glanced over at where the steeldust was tethered, licked his lips, and took three short choppy steps to his left, upslope.

Glencannon said at length, "Who bruised you up like that? Brewer, maybe?"

"That ain't none of your business."

"It is if Brewer's involved."

"You . . . you're the one at the Dollar Wagon last night. The one who knocked out Jess —" The kid broke off abruptly, swallowed again, and took another step upslope. He was within a half-dozen paces of Glencannon now.

"Jess? How come you know the monte dealer's name?"

Barber shook his head. Then he checked himself and said, "I . . . I met him once before."

"You happen to meet Jersey Jack Halacy before too?"

"No . . ."

"Maybe you have. In fact, maybe you work for him."

"No!"

"As a shill for that monte game," Glencannon said.

Another headshake, almost desperate this time. "I told you, no. Listen, you got no call to question me like this. I don't know nothin' about Halacy and the Dollar Wagon. I don't know nothin' about your friend Clay Brewer."

Glencannon glanced up at the bright hazy sky. There were four buzzards down the way now, still wheeling, still making their ugly chatter. "How about those buzzards down there?" he said grimly. "You know anything about them?"

Without warning, the kid made a break for his horse. Glencannon had been poised for some kind of move, but Barber was faster than he'd expected and greased-pig slippery. He lunged after the kid, got a hand on him as Barber swung up into leather, then lost the grip as the gangly tow-head twisted and kicked out with one leg. The pointed toe of his boot caught Glencannon a glancing blow on the neck, spun him around and staggered him. Glencannon's feet went out from under him; he landed hard on his buttocks and skidded a short ways downslope before he

51

could bring himself up.

By the time he scrambled to his feet, Barber had wheeled his steeldust out of the clearing and was gone. The sound of pounding hoofbeats thudded, fading, on the still, hot air. Glencannon thought briefly of giving chase, but the steeldust had looked faster than his own sorrel, and with the lead the kid had the odds were against running him down. And even if he did manage to run him down, what then? He had no more proof of wrongdoing against him than he had against Halacy and his Dollar Wagon crew.

Besides, there were those buzzards nearby. He had to know what they were after; he had to either confirm or deny his suspicions.

He slapped angrily at his clothing, went to where the sorrel had stopped to graze, and swung up. The scar of his missing ear had begun to itch; he rubbed at it with the same anger and frustration. Then he took the horse back onto the rocky trail, down it toward the hungry voices of the carrion birds.

A hundred rods along, the trail veered away from the river. At this point there was a jumble of rocks and thorny scrub-brush that hid the sluggish line of water beyond. Glencannon pulled up. The buzzards flew their crazy patterns almost directly overhead, down toward the river. And there were signs — broken branches, the scrape mark of a horse's shoe on one of the rocks — that somebody had been through the tangle recently. Somebody like Barber, with his shirt studded with burrs and grasstails.

Purse-mouthed, Glencannon eased the sorrel off the trail and down to the river. The brush scratched at him, put burrs on his own shirt and trouser legs. It took him the better part of five minutes to make his way to where he could see both the water's edge and a place along it where a mound of stones, low and rounded and vaguely pyramid-shaped, rose from the cracked earth. One of the damned buzzards was sitting on top of the rocks when Glencannon broke through; but then it wheeled upward, screeching, and joined the others circling above.

The sight of the rocks made his mood dark and dangerous. He drew the Peacemaker, fired three rounds at the buzzards. Tailfeathers flew from one but it didn't fall; all of them climbed higher and floated there out of range, looking down at him with their malevolent red eyes as he dismounted and went over to the mound of rocks.

It was a grave, all right. And a carelessly made one, because part of a booted leg was visible on the river side. Cursing, Glencannon began to unpile the rocks, hurling them out of the way until he uncovered the body that lay beneath. It was lying face down, but the head was turned into profile. And the shirtback was stiff with dried blood.

Clay Brewer had been shot in the back at least three times.

Five

Struggling to keep his emotions under control, Glencannon turned Brewer over and knelt looking into the empty face. Muscles relaxed in death, it wore no particular expression; the wide staring eyes were blank, showing none of the pain and shock Brewer must have felt at the closing instant of his life.

Backshot, Glencannon thought. He stared down at the empty holster on Brewer's hip; the Dragoon Colt was gone. Halacy or one of those other sons of bitches had backshot him and stolen his gun, and then they'd sent the kid into town to fetch his horse from the livery and get rid of it somewhere. Make it look like Brewer had run off, or met with an accident of some kind in which his body never turned up; that was the idea. Then the kid had been sent out here to bury him in a place nobody was likely to come looking. Come the fall rains, the river would have swollen to cover the gravesite and kept it covered until next summer — an added protection against discovery.

But they'd made two mistakes. One was sending a scared and not too bright kid like Barber to do their dirty work. The other was killing a man when he had a friend like

Glencannon around.

Gently, he brushed the dirt off Brewer's face and then closed the eyelids for the last time. He lifted the body, grunting with effort, and carried it to the sorrel, where he hoisted it belly down behind the saddle. The horse stirred skittishly, scenting death; Glencannon paused to stroke its nose, say a few soothing words. Then he uncoiled his saddle rope and used it to tie the body in place, wishing that he had a blanket or the slicker in his saddlebags back at The Mason House, so he could cover it from the heat and from the staring eyes back in Wild Horse.

Mounting, he took the horse slowly back through the underbrush to the trail. When he reached the fork he had to stop and readjust the position of the body. He met no one on the wagon road, and when he passed Willow Flat he saw that the Dollar Wagon was still there but that there was no sign of Halacy and the others. Maybe they'd gone into town; the three saddle horses were no longer grazing nearby. Glencannon hoped so. He wanted to be along when Sheriff Oldham confronted them, and the sooner that happened, the better he'd like it.

It was mid-afternoon when he entered Wild Horse on Place Street, across part of the rail line that shimmered with heat toward opaque horizons. Both Placer and Range Avenue were quiet, somnolent under the blazing sun. Only a few pedestrians trod the plank sidewalks, keeping to the shaded store-front porches as much as possible; some of those stopped to stare as he passed them by, shading their eyes from the sunglare. A pair of riders moved by him, horses' hooves stirring up whorls of dust, their hats tucked low, and both of them also gaped at the dead man. But Glencannon kept his eyes straight ahead and the sorrel at the slow walk until he neared a low white-washed frame building in the block south of the jail.

He'd noticed the frame building earlier, and the pole sign in the dry grass in front that read: *Flagg's Funeral Parlor.* An alleyway ran alongside it, wide enough for a hearse wagon, showing wheel ruts in the hardpacked earth. Glencannon turned into the alley. He was just starting past the front corner, toward a double-doored side entrance, when one of the doors opened and a man wearing a mortician's frock coat hurried out.

The man's small bright eyes watched Glencannon eagerly as he dismounted, darting between him and the trussed remains of Clay Brewer. "Ah, too bad, too bad," he said in a mournful voice. But he didn't sound regretful; he only sounded eager. "Was it an accident?"

"No," Glencannon said. "Help me get him untied and inside."

"Certainly. Right away."

The mortician, whose name turned out to be Alonzo Flagg, fluttered around while Glencannon unknotted the rope. A small knot of people had gathered out on Range Avenue and were standing in front of the alley, gawking. Glencannon yelled out at them, "Somebody get the sheriff. There's been a killing."

Two boys just into their teens broke away from the others and began to run upstreet toward the jail. Glencannon finished untying the body and took hold of Brewer's slack arms; Flagg grasped the legs. Together they carried the body inside and laid it out on a heavy wooden table.

Flagg wrinkled his nose as he stepped back. "He's a mite ripe. How long has he been dead?"

"Since last night sometime."

"Well, we'll have to get him boxed and buried soon. Another day in this heat and he won't be fit for a decent burial."

"That's not up to me," Glencannon said shortly. He turned away from the mortician and went back through the open half of the double doors.

When he emerged into the alley he saw Harrison Oldham running toward him from Range Avenue. He also saw that the sheriff wasn't alone; two others were hurrying along at his heels.

Laurie and Dale Brewer.

Glencannon stopped in his tracks, feeling anguish cut through him. Damn! He didn't want to face Clay's family yet — not now, not like this. He felt awkward, helpless; he had no words to deal with tragedy, he didn't know how to go about breaking the bitter news he had brought.

Oldham was glowering as he lumbered up. "So it's you," he said sourly. "What's going on here?"

"Jim! Jim Glencannon!" Laurie had halted beside the sheriff and was looking at Glencannon with a mixture of surprise, pleasure, and fear.

He managed to say, "Hello, Laurie," but he couldn't hold her gaze. He looked past her at the small crowd on Range Avenue, ran a self-conscious hand over the scar of his missing ear.

Oldham demanded, "What's this about a killing, Glencannon? You go and shoot somebody after I turned you loose?"

"No."

"Well? Who's the dead man you brought in?"

Glencannon hesitated. But Laurie, looking at him intently, must have read the truth in his face. One of her hands came up and clutched at her face and she said, "Oh God!" in a tremulous voice. "Jim, it's . . . it's Clay, isn't it? It's Clay . . ."

The anguish cut at him again. Conflicting emotions swirled through him; he would have given anything to be a hundred miles away at this moment, and yet at the same time he yearned to be able to go to her, take her in his arms, comfort her.

He swallowed and found the words that had to be said. "Yes, it's Clay. I'm sorry, Laurie."

She didn't cry or show any other sign of breaking down; she was a strong woman and always had been. Her only reaction was to squeeze her eyes shut. The boy, Dale, put his arm around her shoulders and held her awkwardly. His jaw trembled and his young face was twisted with grief, but a kindling rage blazed in his green eyes.

None of them moved or spoke for several seconds. Even Oldham held his peace. Then Dale let go of his mother and stepped over in front of Glencannon. Except for dark auburn hair he had inherited from Laurie, and a quiet, almost bookish nature, he was the image of Clay Brewer as a young man: big, powerfully built, with hands the size of small spades.

"Who did it?" he asked, his voice husky with feeling. "Who killed my pa?"

Again Glencannon hesitated.

"I want to know," Dale said. His huge hands clenched, unclenched, clenched again. "I won't let him get away with it, whoever he is. I'll —"

"You won't do anything, son," Oldham said. "That's my job. Now you just take it easy. And see to your ma while Glencannon and me have a little talk."

Dale started to protest, then changed his mind and clamped his mouth tight shut. But the fury still blazed unchecked in his eyes. He stepped back alongside Laurie, stood stiffly with hands still clenching and unclenching at his sides.

Laurie said, "I want to see him."

"That's your right, Miz Brewer," Oldham told her. "But I'd best take the first look myself.

Come on, Glencannon. We'll talk inside."

The sheriff started over to the side entrance. Before following, Glencannon let his gaze linger on Laurie's face. In spite of himself he felt a different kind of ache underneath the anguish inside him. She looked much as he remembered her from his last visit: younger than her years, a touch heavier which only added to her mature beauty, hair the same flawless and fiery flow across her shoulders. Yet time *had* blurred his memory some. He had forgotten just how soft her hair looked, just how brown and compelling were her eyes . . .

Inside the funeral parlor, Oldham shooed Flagg away from the body by telling him that the dead man's kinfolk were outside. The mortician, trailing a cloth measuring-tape from one hand, hurried away into the alley. Then the sheriff made a slow circuit of the table, studying the lifeless shell stretched out there.

"Shot in the back," he said at length. He cocked an eyebrow at Glencannon. "How'd it happen?"

"I don't know for sure. I wasn't there."

"Uh-huh. Dust and dirt all over him. Where'd you find the body?"

"Buried under some rocks along the river," Glencannon said, "a half-mile or so south of town."

"Where you just happened to be digging for gold, eh?"

"I was out looking for Brewer, on my way to

60

his ranch, and there were buzzards circling around in the area. They led me to the gravesite."

"Buzzards," Oldham said dryly.

"That's right. The kid left part of the body exposed when he buried it."

"Kid? What kid is that?"

"A tow-head named Barber. He was at the Dollar Wagon last night, playing in the monte game."

"And you think this kid killed Brewer, is that it?"

"Not exactly. I think it was Jersey Jack Halacy or one of his Dollar Wagon crew."

"The hell you say."

"The hell I don't say." Glencannon proceeded to tell the sheriff everything he knew and suspicioned about Brewer's murder, including his encounters with the Dollar Wagon bunch at Willow Flat and with the tow-head near the gravesite.

"That's a pip of a story," Oldham said when Glencannon was finished. Skepticism was plain in his voice. "With or without the buzzards."

Glencannon managed to hold his temper. "Sorry I can't dress it up more to your liking."

"A *pip* of a story, just the same."

"Listen, are you going to arrest Halacy and his crew?"

"On what grounds? Your say-so?"

"I'm telling you, they're the ones who killed Brewer!"

"And I'm tellin' *you,* you got no proof to back up that accusation. You weren't there when Brewer was shot, you admitted that yourself. You don't know where it happened, or when, or how. Halacy and his boys didn't admit anything to you and neither did the kid."

"The kid didn't have to admit anything. He's guilty as sin; it was written all over his face —"

"You say."

"For Christ's sake, talk to the old man at the livery stable! He'll tell you it was the kid who came around this morning to fetch Brewer's horse."

"What'll that prove?" Oldham said. "This tow-head told you Brewer give him a dollar gold piece to fetch the horse; it could've happened that way. And Brewer could have been ambushed, or gotten himself into some kind of ruckus, after he left town this morning."

"Damn it, sheriff, Brewer was killed last night, probably out at Willow Flat. Find the kid, put that to him yourself. Pressure him enough and he'll spill everything."

"If he's still around, I'll find him. Then we'll see."

"What about Halacy?"

"What about him?"

"You're at least going to question him?"

"I reckon I am."

"When?"

"When I get to it. Don't try to tell me how to do my job, son. I don't like it much."

Glencannon started to say something else, bitterly, but Alonzo Flagg came back in just then. "Excuse me, sheriff," he said, "but I've got to get right to work. Mrs. Brewer has asked me to go ahead with funeral preparations."

"You didn't bother her, did you?" Glencannon snapped at him.

"Bother? Me? No, sir! I only explained the necessity for a rapid Christian burial, because of the heat and the nature of Mr. Brewer's, ah, demise. Mrs. Brewer agreed that an immediate burial would be best for all concerned."

"Nobody's buryin' nobody until I say so," Oldham said.

"But sheriff, time is of the essence. Another day and his kinfolk won't be able to come near the body for the smell."

"I want Doc Simpkins to take a look at it first."

"All right, fine," the mortician said. "Can't he do that in the next hour or so?"

"Well, I expect he can."

Glencannon wanted to shout at them to shut up, that Clay Brewer had been his friend and a decent human being and they had no right to talk as if he'd never been anything more than a chunk of half-spoiled meat. But he knew how pointless and foolish that would be. This was a hard country, sometimes an ugly one, and death had to be treated with the same practicality as anything else. There was no time for sentiment, especially not in the heat and drought of summer, when there was no ice to preserve foodstuffs, let alone the body of a dead man.

"Go on over and bring the Doc," Oldham was saying to Alonzo Flagg. "I'll wait here until you get back."

"Then can I get on with my preparations?"

"I reckon." The sheriff turned to Glencannon as Flagg hurried into the front of the funeral parlor. "As for you, Glencannon, you keep yourself where I can find you easy. We ain't had our last talk yet."

"How about if I go with you to see Halacy?"

"Uh-uh. You get riled up too quick. I'll handle Halacy myself, just like I'll handle everything else in this business."

Arguing wouldn't get him anywhere; Glencannon could see that. He clamped his teeth together and stalked out into the alley, leaving Oldham alone with the body.

Laurie and Dale were still standing there, being consoled now by three women in sunbonnets and faded gingham. Laurie seemed to be bearing up, although her expression was still one of shock and grief. The boy kept shifting his weight from one foot to the other, as if impatient to be elsewhere, doing something to work off his own feelings of loss. His eyes were still angry, but controlled now, the glow in them like that of a banked fire.

When Laurie saw Glencannon emerge she broke away from the three women and came over to him. "Jim? Can I see him now?"

"Do you have to?"

"Yes," she said, "I have to."

He nodded wordlessly.

Dale said, "I'm going in with you, ma."

"Of course you are. He's your father." She looked again at Glencannon. "Will you wait here for us, Jim? So we can talk?"

"You know I will."

With Dale at her side, Laurie walked stiff-legged into the funeral parlor; the door closed behind her. Glencannon stared at it, conscious for the first time in hours of the throbbing pain in his head. When he finally turned away he saw that the three sun-bonneted women were watching him with open curiosity, as were others at the mouth of the alleyway. He ignored them all, put his back to them and led his sorrel to the far end of the alley, where a wooden fence marked the rear of Alonzo Flagg's property. Then he rolled a cigarette and tried not to think about what he'd have to say to Laurie and Dale when they came out again.

Six

Clay Brewer's funeral was held near sundown, while streaks of orange, pink and lavender still highlighted the western horizon.

There were four wagons and a single horse-and-rider in the procession that crossed the narrow wooden bridge at River Street and traveled through the rosy dusk to the graveyard west of town. The lead wagon, painted a dull stovepipe black, with a fringed canopy over driver and bed as shelter from the ravages of sun and storm, bore Brewer's remains in a plain coffin. On the hearse's hard seat Alonzo Flagg shifted uncomfortably, as if wishing the trip was over, but he allowed his two mares to pull at their own pace, for haste would only have raised billowing dust clouds to choke the others behind. Glencannon held the reins on the seat of the Brewers' open ranch buggy, with Laurie, her body bent and her head bowed, sitting at his side. The third wagon belonged to Reverend John Flynn, Wild Horse's combination minister and schoolteacher, and the fourth to a couple named Pitchfield who lived near the Brewers and had been in town that afternoon. The lone rider was Dale. He had ridden his roan gelding into town earlier, while his mother drove the buggy, and he had insisted on riding it to the cemetery.

The graveyard was located on a grassy knoll, the grass brown and parched now, overlooking both the river and the town. The two men who had been hired by Flagg as gravediggers were resting in the shade of a willow tree when the procession arrived. They scrambled to their feet as the undertaker braked his hearse, and helped Glencannon and Dale carry the coffin to the open grave.

Reverend Flynn, a devout man with a bristly gray moustache and a prominently veined nose, intoned several prayers and other tributes to the heavenly home to which he bequeathed Clay Brewer's immortal soul. As he did so the men, with the aid of ropes, lowered Brewer to his final resting place, his head to the east, his feet to the west. The casket had been cloaked with a piece of black cheesecloth; the cloth fluttered in the faint evening breeze, as did the open pages of the Good Book in the minister's hand.

"Man that is born of woman hath but a short time to live, and is full of misery . . ."

Laurie stood as if stunned, her face drained of color, her eyes moist. Dale's face, like Glencannon's, was impassive, but emotions roiled beneath the surface; Glencannon could see that whenever he glanced at the boy, and it made him edgy. It was plain how Dale felt, even though he had said little since looking at his father in the funeral parlor. He felt the same way himself —

dangerously wired up, ready to lash out in a release of anger and frustration.

"We therefore commit his body to the ground, earth to earth, ashes to ashes, dust to dust . . ." The minister knelt as he read aloud, scooped up a handful of dirt, and sprinkled it symbolically into the grave. ". . . is able to subdue all things to himself, amen." Stepping back, he stowed his frayed prayerbook inside his dark coat. "You can close it up now, lads."

Before the diggers could start, Glencannon wrenched one of the shovels away and furiously assaulted the pile of dirt. Sod thudded dully on the coffin, beginning to blanket the cheesecloth. Seconds later Dale moved forward, caught up the second shovel, and joined him. Laurie remained motionless by the grave, until Reverend Flynn crossed and escorted her to her buggy; the others backed away to stand alongside the hearse.

When Glencannon and Dale finished mounding the grave they erected a plain white cross, supplied by Flynn, at its head. Wielding the shovel had been an outlet for some of the violence inside Glencannon; he felt less wired up now, more in control of himself. The same seemed to be true of Dale, he saw as he used his hat to slap dust from his hands. The anger in the youth's eyes was once again banked.

They both went to where Laurie waited at the buggy. Dale said, "I'm going to ride on ahead, ma. I need to be alone for a spell."

"All right, son."

Glencannon watched the boy mount his roan and ride out of the cemetery, into the purpling darkness. Then he handed Laurie onto the wagon seat, said to Reverend Flynn, "A nice service, preacher," and climbed up beside her. Alonzo Flagg was already at the reins of the hearse; as soon as he wheeled it around and headed out, Glencannon took the buggy in behind. The Pitchfields and the minister followed a short time later.

For some minutes Glencannon drove without speaking. Laurie sat stiffly composed, her eyes fixed straight ahead, unblinking. He stole sidelong glances at her, trying to decide whether her silence and her composure were signs of strength or of something else. She had been like this all day, even while he was explaining what he believed had happened to Clay. It just didn't seem natural, somehow.

"What are you thinking, Jim?"

She had turned her head toward him; her face shone whitely, half-shadowed, in the early moonlight. "I was thinking about you."

"You mean the way I'm taking Clay's death. No tears, no display of emotion."

"Well . . . yes."

"That's because I've changed, Jim. I'm not the same woman I was the last time you visited."

"All of us change," Glencannon said.

"Not you. You're a little older, but that's all."

He shook his head. "I've changed too, Laurie.

69

It's something a man can't avoid. Or a woman. Besides, still water turns stagnant."

She made a small odd sound in her throat. "Stagnant," she said. "Yes, that's the right word for it."

"Why do you say it like that? You're not stagnant."

"Maybe not any more."

"Clay?"

"Yes. Clay." She was facing him squarely now, and Glencannon was startled by the depth of unhappiness that had opened up in her gaze. "But it's not right to speak ill of the dead, is it?"

He was silent for a moment. Then he said, "Let it out if you feel the need. It can't hurt Clay, but keeping it in and letting it fester can only hurt you."

Again that small sound, almost a whisper. "It was the baby dying," she said. "He wanted that little girl more than anything in the world, and he couldn't seem to reconcile himself to the loss. He blamed me, he blamed himself, he even blamed Dale. And the fact that the ranch wasn't doing well only made things worse. He turned sullen, started drinking and gambling more than was right, neglecting chores, neglecting . . . everything. He . . . he stopped being a father to Dale or a husband to me."

"He didn't mistreat you?"

"No, not the way you mean. He never laid hand to either of us. Never laid hand to me at all." She took a deep breath. "Our marriage wasn't a marriage for the past year."

"You mean — ?"

"Yes. Ever since the baby died."

Glencannon didn't know what to say. Awkwardness took hold of him; he felt big and helpless sitting there beside her. And conscious of her nearness at the same time. He lifted one hand from the reins, rubbed it over the bandage on his head, over the scar of his missing ear.

"It's awkward for you," she said. She had always been a perceptive woman, as well as a strong one. "Maybe I shouldn't have said anything."

"No, it's all right. I'm sorry, Laurie."

"So am I. But Clay was my choice, after all, and we shared good times together that I'll remember long after the rest has faded."

They had crossed the bridge at River Street and were nearing Range Avenue now. Most of the buildings showed lamplight and there was a good scatter of traffic along the boardwalks. The carnival hullabaloo of the previous night was being repeated; Glencannon could hear shouts, laughter, the tinny music of pianos in the Range Avenue saloons. And he loathed Wild Horse in that moment, resenting its waste of what little happiness there was in this world, while Laurie was denied even a small share of it.

When they turned onto Range Avenue Glencannon glanced southward, to the wide clearing beyond the livery stable. The Dollar Wagon was there, as he had expected it would be, and if anything the crowd clustered around it was larger than it had been last night. Lantern light bathed it, letting him see the tall, fancy-dressed figure of Jersey Jack Halacy standing on the wagon seat and delivering his spiel. The monte barrels were also visible at the rear. Glencannon felt anger crowd in on him again. And this time it was directed as much at Sheriff Harrison Oldham as at Halacy and his Dollar Wagon crew. Had Oldham even bothered to talk to them? Had he made any effort at all to find the kid, Barber?

Dale was waiting in front of the funeral parlor, standing with his roan and staring downstreet toward the Dollar Wagon. Glencannon took the buggy up alongside him, as Flagg's hearse turned into the alleyway, and drew rein.

"It's getting late," he said to Laurie. "You and Dale are planning to stay over, aren't you?"

"No, I don't think so. The town is so . . . wild tonight. I couldn't stand that, Jim."

"But it's a long ride out to your place —"

"I know, but I'll have Dale with me. And the Pitchfields. We'll be home by midnight."

Glencannon stepped down, gave Laurie his arm. Joining them, Dale asked his mother, "Are we going to the ranch, ma?"

"Yes." She looked at Glencannon. "You'll come out to see us, won't you, Jim? Tomorrow?"

"You couldn't keep me away."

"Meantime you won't . . . do anything foolish?"

"About Halacy and his bunch? No."

"I've lost my husband. I don't want to lose my best friend."

"You won't lose me, don't worry. Dale, you take care of your ma, hear?"

"I will," the youth said quietly. "I'll take care of everything now that pa's gone."

Glencannon waited until Laurie and Dale and the Pitchfields were on their way. Then he hunted up Alonzo Flagg inside the funeral parlor and paid him part of the cost of Clay Brewer's funeral, promising to deliver the rest in the morning. Laurie had little money, and he was flush with King Rowan's wages and bonus; he felt it was the least he could do. For her, for Dale, and for the memory of his murdered friend.

From there he made straight for the jail in the next block. The lamps were lit inside; he shoved open the door without knocking and went inside. Sheriff Oldham was there, leaning hipshot against a corner of his desk, talking to a youngish man wearing a cutaway coat and a brace of .44 Remingtons cross-draw fashion underneath. Both of them looked over at Glencannon, and the sheriff's mouth turned down at the corners to match the droop of his mustaches.

"You again," he said sourly.

"That's right, sheriff. Me again."

"Well? What is it this time?"

Glencannon hesitated, glancing at the other man.

"This here's Ed Riggins," Oldham said. "He's my deputy. You can say whatever you have to in front of him."

"You know what I'm here about. Did you find Barber?"

"No, I didn't."

"Did you do much looking?"

"Now wait a minute —" Riggins began, but Oldham cut him off.

"I did plenty of looking, son. But that kid is either long gone or holed up somewhere that nobody knows about. I can't talk to a man I can't find, and I can't arrest him neither. Even if it turns out he needs arrestin', which you're positive of but I ain't."

"Halacy and his crew are easy enough to find," Glencannon said thinly.

"Sure they are. And I found 'em and talked to 'em too, just like I said I would."

"And?"

"And nothing. Halacy claims he don't know Barber and the other three back him up. Says he never seen Clay Brewer after the ruckus last night, either."

"You believe him, I suppose."

"Ain't no reason to disbelieve him."

"You seem to disbelieve me, though."

"Well, son, you only been in Wild Horse twenty-four hours and already you been mixed up in a brawl, spent the night in jail, and carted in the body of a murdered man. That's a heap more trouble than Halacy's made in all the visits

74

he's made combined."

Glencannon's hands fisted at his sides. *You old son of a bitch,* he thought. *You're some lawman, you are. Useless as tits on a billygoat.* But as much as he'd have liked to, he didn't put any of this into words; it would only have landed him back in a cell, and this time he wouldn't be able to buy his way out in the morning.

"All right, Oldham," he said, "have it your way. But if you won't see justice done, then I'll have to see to it myself."

"Hold on now," the sheriff said, and his voice had hardened. "You ain't fixin' to go off half-cocked, are you? Doin' something crazy like facin' down Halacy and his boys yourself?"

"If that's what it takes for justice, maybe I am."

"Not in my town, son. You make any more trouble here, you'll wish you hadn't."

"And that's no bull, either," Riggins added coldly.

Glencannon had nothing more to say; he spun on his heel and launched out onto the boardwalk.

His first thought as he pounded away from the jail was to head down to the Dollar Wagon; but in his frame of mind, he'd only be hell-bent for trouble. What he needed most of all right now was a drink to calm himself down. He found his way to the Ace High Saloon, bellied up to the bar, and called for a double rye with a beer chaser. When he had the drinks under his belt he felt less inclined to pay a call on the Dollar Wagon, and less inclined to rush out after vengeance. That was what Clay Brewer had done and he'd bought three bullets in the back for his carelessness. No, the smart thing was to move along slow and careful, try to find Barber himself, or some other kind of evidence against Halacy and his bunch.

He decided that he'd best head back to The Mason House and make sure he still had a room for the night and that his saddlebags and the rest of his money were still safe. A shave and a bath would do him good too. Then, afterward, he could move around town and see what there was to learn.

He left the Ace High, walked up to the hotel. The stiff-faced clerk was behind the desk, reading another dime novel — something called *Deadwood Dick, the Prince of the Road; or the Black Rider of the Black Hills* — by the light of the desk lamp. He looked up as Glencannon approached, laid the book down, and pushed the register around.

"Thought you'd be back, mister," he said. "Planning to stay another night?"

"That's right."

"Just sign the register." The clerk peered at him through his spectacles as Glencannon took up the pen. "Like I said, I figured you'd be back. What with your belongings still upstairs and all. That's what I told the young fellow when he came around looking for you."

Glencannon stopped writing and straightened up, scowling. "What young fellow?" he demanded.

"I don't know his name. Young tow-head off the street, looked like he'd been in a fight. Had bruises on his face, you know?"

"Yeah," Glencannon said, "I know. What'd he want?"

"You."

Glencannon waited. So did the clerk. Glencannon dug into his Levi's and slapped a silver piece on the counter. The clerk picked it up and tapped it against his front teeth, then pocketed it and said, "He came in about an hour and a half ago. Seemed excited about something. He left a message for you."

"What message?"

"He wants you to meet him at the livery stable at one a.m."

"Why? What for?"

"He said it had something to do with the Dollar Wagon."

"Is that all?"

"That's all," the clerk said. He reached behind him for Glencannon's key. "You happen to be a gambling man, Mr. Glencannon?"

"That depends. Why?"

"It's early yet, is all; three hours before midnight. If you're looking for a way to pass the time, I just thought you might like to try the Dollar Wagon. I understand they run a nice, friendly game of monte down there."

Seven

Glencannon approached the livery stable from the rear.

It was fifteen minutes before one a.m. The livery, which had closed at midnight, was dark; so was the clearing beyond, where the Dollar Wagon had stood until it, too, by city ordinance, had shut down at midnight and headed out of town, evidently to camp again at Willow Flat. Glencannon had taken up a hiding place behind a board fence at the rear of the corral, coming there some minutes before midnight, and from the shadows he'd watched the Wagon leave. Halacy had been driving it, with the monte dealer, Jess, on the seat beside him; the other two rode saddle horses and trailed along behind. Since then, the only people he'd seen had been a drunk with a bottle, lurching away toward the river, and the deputy sheriff, Riggins, on routine rounds checking the stable's front and side entrances.

But Glencannon still maintained his caution as he eased along the fence and, keeping close to a stretch of weedy brush, worked his way toward the stable. Maybe Barber's request to see him was legitimate, maybe the kid had had a change of heart and wanted to make a clean breast of his involvement with Halacy and the murder of Clay Brewer, but Glencannon had his doubts. It seemed a little too pat for his liking; and a private meeting at this time of night had the smell of a trap. Could be that Halacy had put the tow-head up to it, worried, maybe, that Glencannon was stirring up too much trouble. If that was it, it meant Jersey Jack was running scared, and a scared man was much more likely to make mistakes. The kind of mistakes, Glencannon reflected grimly, that would lead him straight to the gallows.

He would have liked to have the law here with him, no matter what the situation turned out to be. A witness, and a back-up gun, would be to his benefit. But with Oldham's attitude being what it was, he had decided against inviting the sheriff in on this party. Oldham might not have come in the first place, or he might have wanted to handle things differently and maybe scared off Barber and anyone else who might show up. Like it or not, he had to play a lone hand.

He moved along the split-rail corral fence, to where it abutted a small tool shed attached to the stable. The slight evening breeze had long since died; heat from the day still hung cloying in the moonlit gray night. Sweat sheened his face, formed little runnels that trickled down into the collar of his shirt. The palm of his right hand was slick where it rested on the butt of his Colt Peacemaker.

The shadows alongside the stable were thick,

obscuring the side entrance; some of them were cast by the building itself and some by a pair of willows and a large horse chestnut tree that grew nearby. The nearest lamplight was a block away, in one window of the church beyond Range Avenue. Noise still came from the saloons further uptown, but it was muted now, no longer raucous, because most of the farmers and cowhands had either left town or turned in for the night. Here where Glencannon was, the silence was thick, unbroken.

He hunkered down in the pocket of blackness formed by the joining of the stable and the shed, eased his Colt out of its holster and laid it across his knee. More minutes crawled past. A night coach with side lanterns lit, rocking in its thoroughbraces, clattered past on Range Avenue and then disappeared on Placer. A locomotive whistle keened the night uptown at the rail yards; the faint banging of couplers and grinding of brake shoes drifted on the heat-choked air. But there was still no sign of Barber or anybody else in the vicinity.

Glencannon began to fidget. He shifted position, shifted it again, and finally stood up and laid his back against the shed wall. A heavy rumbling started up behind him to the north and he heard again the wail of the train whistle, coming closer now. The line of tracks and the banks of dry grass between the stable and the river grew day-bright; then the black silhouette of an engine, its headlamp shining like a giant's eye, hove into view, dragging a string of six loaded cattle cars, two boxcars, and a caboose. As the freight clacked past, Glencannon used his left hand to slide out his old stem-winder and lift the covers. By holding it up close to his eyes he could read the time. It was seven minutes past one o'clock.

Damn it, where the hell was Barber?

When the freight curled out over the railroad trestle that spanned the river south of town, Glencannon hunkered down again in the shadows. Maybe this business wasn't a trap after all, he thought. Maybe it was the real thing and the kid had lost his nerve at the last minute and called it off. A false alarm was the last goddamn thing —

Somebody came around the front corner of the stable.

Glencannon stiffened, pulled back hard against the shed wall. But there was no stealth in the way the dark figure moved, or at least not the kind that indicated he was trying to remain unseen. He came forward slowly, moving out away from the stable wall, and then stopped a dozen paces from the side entrance; he was jerky on his feet, the way a man gets when he's nervous or excited. He cast looks around him, turning his body as he did so. Enough moonlight filtered through the nearby trees and tinged the shadows to let Glencannon recognize the towhead. And to let him see that both of Barber's hands were empty of weapons.

Glencannon let another three or four minutes pass. Nothing changed in the tableau in front of him; the kid continued to move jerkily in the same place, looking this way and that, and his hands stayed away from his gun belt. All right, Glencannon thought. He eased forward out of the thick shadows, glided forward along the stable wall.

He was almost to the side entrance before the kid heard the whisper of his bootsoles in the dust. Barber whirled, but he didn't make to draw his gun; instead he spread his arms out away from his body, stood dead-still as if holding his breath. Glencannon came past the side door and stopped a few feet in front of the kid. He made sure to hold the Peacemaker up where moonlight glinted off the barrel and Barber could see it.

"You're late," Glencannon said. "I've been waiting a hell of a long time."

The kid said in a trembly voice, "I'm here now. Ready."

"Ready for what? To tell the truth about —"

There was a sudden sliding sound behind him. Glencannon bit off the words, started to swing both his body and the Peacemaker around. He had a quick perception of the side door to the stable standing open, of a black-garbed figure lunging toward him; then something cracked down across his neck, staggered him, drove him to his knees. Pain erupted, sent pinwheels of light flashing across his vision and left him dazed, only half-conscious.

A voice floated to him out of the confusion. "Luke, what're you doin'?" it said, and it sounded choked with fear. "No, Luke, for God's sake, *no!*"

Then there was a muffled explosion that seemed to come to Glencannon from a long way off. It echoed and re-echoed, until another voice drowned it out, this one saying, "This is for you, you bastard." As if in a dream, he felt a hand yank his Colt from his nerveless fingers, only to return it again seconds later. He tried to shake his head clear, to rise, but the voice said, "This is for you too," and more pain erupted, a savage snapping pain along the point of his jaw. He felt himself falling, falling —

Then he stopped falling and the blackness swept over him.

It was a long time before he came out of it. And when he did, nausea swept through him, made him flop over on his belly and vomit. Weakly, he dragged himself onto all fours and knelt there gasping, pawing at his mouth, gritting his teeth against the agony in his head and neck.

Another minute or so passed before the pain subsided enough to let him think. He hauled back on his knees, groaning, and forced his eyes open. It was still night, but the darkness was beginning to gray a little at the edges: less than an hour before dawn. He lifted his left hand, rubbed it along the nape of his neck and felt the warm stickiness of blood caking his hair. There was a weight in his right hand, he realized then, and lifted that to stare at the gun still clenched in his fingers.

It wasn't his; it was a .44 Remington.

He couldn't figure the sense of it at first. Then he remembered the kid, and the voices that had floated to him out of the night, and he understood why the guns had been switched. A mixture of urgency and fear clawed at him; he got one foot under him and managed to lurch upright. When he did that he half-turned, staggering, and saw the body stretched out belly-down in the shadows near the stable wall. He'd been shot at point-blank range; the back of his head was missing.

Glencannon looked away, over to where the stable's side door still stood open. He'd anticipated a trap, all right, but he hadn't expected it to be sprung from inside the stable. That door had been locked — he'd seen the deputy, Riggins, shake it earlier — and so he'd overlooked it. But it had been easy enough for one of Jersey Jack Halacy's men to get inside, probably through the hayloft door on the far side, and wait until the kid maneuvered Glencannon into a position where his back was to the side entrance. The kid hadn't expected it, but the trap was for him too — a way for Halacy to get rid of two troublesome birds at the same time. He'd underestimated that son of a bitch, all right, Glencannon thought. He wouldn't make the same mistake twice.

The thing to do now was to get the hell out of here. He'd been unconscious for at least three hours and it was a miracle he hadn't been found in that time. Go back to the hotel, tend to his head, try to figure out his next move. He started to back away, with the intention of looping around the shed and going back along the corral fence.

"Hold it!" an angry voice yelled from Range Avenue. "Stay right where you are, Glencannon!"

Glencannon threw a look in that direction, wincing, and saw Sheriff Oldham, Riggins, and three other men loping toward him; one of the others was the old hostler, who carried a mill lantern in his right hand. He thought about bolting, decided that would be a damned fool thing to do, and stood his ground.

When the men pounded up to him, the old hostler said, "Told you what I seen, sheriff. Told you the kid was lyin' here dead and this one beside him with a gun in his hand."

Oldham moved over, looked at Barber's body, then came back and glared at Glencannon. "You had to go and do it, didn't you, son? Even after I warned you."

"I didn't kill him," Glencannon said.

"No? You got a gun in your hand, ain't you?"

"It's not my gun. Hell, you can see that. You took mine away last night; it's a Colt Peacemaker, not a Remington."

"You could've had yourself another one stashed away."

"I tell you, it's not my gun."

"Then whose is it, if it ain't yours?"

"A man named Luke. He works for Halacy."

"Back to the Dollar Wagon boys, are we?"

"That's right. Listen, the kid came around to the hotel yesterday afternoon and left a message for me to meet him here at one a.m. Halacy put him up to it." He went on to explain what had happened, how it had all been a double trap to get rid of both Barber and himself.

The sheriff wasn't impressed. Neither was Riggins or the other three men. They all looked at him hard-eyed, believing what their eyes told them, not what he had to say.

Oldham said, "That's another pip of a story. You got any proof to back it up?"

"The clerk at the hotel will tell you about the kid leaving a message —"

"Sure. That much of it is probably true. You met him here tonight, got into an argument, maybe a fight judging from them marks on you, and then you shot him."

"If I shot him, for Christ's sake, why was I lying here unconscious when the hostler came around?"

Riggins said, "Could be you was hurt in the fight. Could be you pulled the trigger on Barber and fell down right afterwards."

Groggy as he was, Glencannon knew what this talk was leading to. If they arrested him, put him in jail, he'd never be a free man again. He'd stand trial as soon as the circuit judge came through, he'd be convicted, and he'd hang. And Jersey Jack Halacy and his bunch would get away scot-free.

"Best hand over that iron, son," Oldham said to him. "Make things easy on yourself —"

"The hell I will," Glencannon said. He threw the Remington up, let it sweep across the group of men before him. They all froze; the old hostler made a clacking noise with his store teeth. "Don't any of you try for your guns. I don't want to shoot anybody, but if it comes to that . . ." He let the sentence hang meaningfully in the muggy night air.

Oldham said, "You're makin' a mistake, son. A mighty big mistake."

"You're the one who's making the mistake, sheriff."

"Hand over that iron and you've still got a chance to get off with a plea of self-defense."

"I didn't kill Barber."

"And I say you did," Riggins said. He was a hothead, the kind that didn't like to be thrown down on and spoiled for a fight when it happened. That made him extra dangerous. "I say you're a murderin' son of a bitch."

"Easy, Ed," Oldham warned.

"Easy, hell! Are we gonna stand by and let this killer get away with —"

"Shut up," Glencannon snapped.

"Not for the likes of you. Joe, Roy — spread out away from him. You too, Sheriff. He can't get all of us before we get him."

"I can get most of you."

"He won't shoot," Riggins said. "He's a god-damn coward. He only back-shoots men he calls his friends and kids in the dark when they ain't expectin' it."

The words stirred the others; even Oldham's face hardened into a look of determination. The old man spat on the ground and backed off, holding his lantern high; he was the only one of them who wasn't armed. The other four began to spread out, one slow step at a time, their hands hovering near their holstered weapons.

Glencannon only had one choice. He didn't want to kill any of these men, even in self-defense; if he did, then he was sure to hang for murder. Without warning, he lunged toward the sheriff, who was nearest to him and blocking a direct path to the open stable door, and sent Oldham sprawling into the dust. Before any of the others could stop him, or get their guns clear of leather, he ran crouching into the stable and slammed the door shut behind him.

There was a heavy wooden bar drawn back into an iron slot alongside the door; Glencannon caught hold of it, shoved it across the door and into another slot on the opposite side. A hard shoulder rammed into the wood seconds later, bounced off. Then a volley of shots peppered the door, sent Glencannon hurrying back deeper into the darkness.

The stable smelled of horses and leather, sweat and manure. Moonlight trickled through slits in the plankboard walls, letting him see enough of his surroundings to move without stumbling over things. Halters and hackamores and bridles hung from wall pegs, the hayloft made a mass of blurred shadow above, mounds of hay and a scatter of tools, along with a blacksmith's forge and a wagon with one wheel off, cluttered the floor space. There were eight stalls, four of them occupied; the horses moved skittishly in their stalls, alerted by the gunshots outside.

Glencannon stood near the wagon, listening. He could hear shouts, movements, through the thin walls. Spreading out to cover all sides, he thought. And in the meantime, the old hostler would likely be on his way to wake up the town and bring help. The longer he stayed in here, the worse his chances. If he had to fight his way out, people were going to get hurt — and he might not make it at all.

He moved toward the stalls, looking for his sorrel; he'd put the animal up here this afternoon, before leaving with Laurie and Dale for Clay Brewer's funeral. When he found the right stall he opened the gate, patted the horse's nose to gentle him, and backed him out. A rack of saddles rose out of the gloom nearby. Glencannon located the one that belonged to him and cinched it into place. Then he grabbed one of the bridles off the wall, slid the bit into the sorrel's mouth.

He led the horse to the barred front doors.

Gentling it again, he left it there with the reins down and made his way back to the side entrance. He eased the bar off the door, and when it was free he threw it to one side, so that it made a loud clatter. Then he jerked the door open hard, backing away as he did so.

From the graying darkness outside, the sheriff's voice shouted, "He's tryin' to get out the side door!"

There were more shouts as the other men converged on the side entrance. Somebody fired a shot through the open doorway. But Glencannon was already back at the front doors by then, swinging up onto the sorrel. He leaned down to jerk loose the brace; then he kicked the doors open, laid his head and body low over the horse's neck, and jabbed his bootheels into the muscled flanks.

They pounded out into the night, cutting at an angle toward Range Avenue. More shouts; guns cracked twice, three times. Two men were running toward him from upstreet, moonlight glinting off the guns in their hands. Glencannon veered away from them, so sharply that he almost staggered the horse; he let up on the reins, giving the animal its head. Behind him one of the running men dropped to one knee and squeezed off a shot. Glencannon felt a sharp pain in his left shoulder, as if he had been burned with a branding iron. There was a momentary blur of shock, then the arm went numb and began to flop at his side. He laid himself lower across the sorrel's neck, fighting the reins with his right hand, and galloped south for Placer Street.

Another volley of shots sounded behind him, but none of these bullets came near him. He neck-reined the horse onto Placer, took it through the loop onto the wagon road leading south out of Wild Horse. There were houses along here, most of them with picket fences and small gardens; lamps were going on in some of them, and a man in a pair of longjohns was standing on a front porch with a rifle in his hands. But he didn't fire at Glencannon as he raced by.

The whole town would be up in arms before long. And inside half an hour, Glencannon thought grimly, Oldham and Riggins would have formed a posse and be on the trail after him. They would also have the telegraph wires singing between Wild Horse and Iron Bend to the south, Sawyer to the west, and that meant he couldn't stay on the main roads. Besides, his dust would send up a billowing signal to the posse tracking him. His only hope lay in cutting off to the southeast, escaping across the dry prairie into the badlands.

The lights of Wild Horse fell away behind the sorrel's pounding hooves. The sky was lightening rapidly now, coming on toward dawn. Ahead Glencannon could see the grassy section along the river called Willow Flats, the smoky glow of a fire and the outlines of the Dollar

Wagon and the pitched wedge-tents nearby. He had a wild impulse to swing in there, face down Halacy and his bunch and finish things right now; it was the only way he could keep from becoming a fugitive. But that would have been suicidal. His wounded arm still flopped uselessly, even though the numbness was fading and he could feel shoots of pain. He couldn't have fought one man, let alone four. Tasting the bitterness of gall, he spurred the sorrel past without slowing.

A quarter-mile south, between Willow Flats and the fork, he veered off the road and made his run straight toward Gold Buttes.

Eight

The vast Dakota prairie lay beneath the early-morning sun like kindling under a firebrand. A wind had arisen some time before, just past sunup, and it blew flame breath across the barren expanse of buffalo grass and sagebrush and three-foot tufts of bluegrass. As early as it was, the temperature was already in the nineties and climbing.

Glencannon squinted ahead, blinking against the sunglare. The line of limestone buttes loomed closer, but just how close he couldn't tell; the ball of the sun seemed balanced atop them and the blazing light played tricks on his eyes, outlining the domes and spires against the sky like the black fangs of a rattler. They couldn't be much more than a mile distant now, he thought. But a mile was a long way to travel on a flagging horse with a posse closing ground behind.

He turned in the saddle to look at the miniature figures, wreathed in dust, that dogged him in the distance. A half-mile or so separated them now. When they'd first come into his sight, less than an hour ago, he had judged them to be at least a mile off. But they had stronger horses and knew the land better than he did; they'd made up time out of Wild Horse and they were making up more of it with each passing minute. His chances of reaching the badlands and finding a place to hide before they caught up to him were not much better than even.

He twisted his head frontally again, and this time the movements made the bullet wound in his left shoulder spasm with pain. The whole of his shirt on that side was stiff with dried blood; more blood, some of it still sticky, stained his shirtsleeve and the fingers of his left hand. He couldn't tell how badly hurt he was, but the pain was tolerable and he didn't seem to be in any immediate danger of passing out. Flesh wound, maybe with the bullet passing on through. It was the least of his worries right now.

The sorrel was running in spurts, slowing until Glencannon dug his heels in, galloping for a hundred rods and then flagging again. Its coat glistened with flecks of lather and it blew heavily through vented nostrils. Glencannon was afraid that it would stumble in one of the prairie dog holes scattered here and there across the flatland, or stagger and collapse from plain exhaustion. He held off flogging the animal, let it run for a time at a retarded pace, and again swiveled his head to look behind him.

The riders were still gaining; if it hadn't been for the spume of dust surrounding them, he would have been able to make out individuals, maybe judge how many there were in the posse. It wouldn't be long before they were within rifle distance. Shooting from the back of a running horse was a tricky business, but that might not stop some of them from trying it.

Far off to his left, he saw then, was another of the hardscrabble ranches he'd passed at a distance since dawn. Smoke rose from its chimney, making a wind-curled pattern on the hazy blue sky. Glencannon wondered briefly if that or one of the others was the Brewer ranch. But it didn't make any difference; he could expect no help from Laurie and Dale, or from anybody else. The nearness of the posse made certain of that.

He squinted ahead at the buttes. They seemed so close now that he could almost reach out and touch them — or were his eyes still playing tricks? No, he was coming into higher ground; he could see it ahead, feel the sorrel slow up even more, its muscles trembling, as it began to labor upward.

The terrain rose rapidly in ragged sweeps. Grass and sagebrush gave way to jumbles of shale and volcanic rock; the sorrel's hooves clattered for the first time against solid stone. The going became as rough as the land, jarring him in the saddle, sending fresh shoots of pain through his arm and neck. The wound in his shoulder began to bleed again. He felt warm liquid flow stickily along his arm, down his side, and all at once a flood of weakness overtook him; he might be close to blacking out after all. His vision was blurred with sweat and dust and strain, and shadows seemed to be gathering at the edges.

There was a cracking sound behind him, pop-gun loud, and a bullet whined off an outcropping thirty yards away.

He pulled his head around, fighting dizziness. The posse was close enough now so that he could see eight riders spread out and climbing after him. One of them had a rifle butted against his shoulder; light erupted from the muzzle and there was another cracking noise. This time the bullet missed closer, snapping twigs off a clump of sagebrush.

Instinctively Glencannon dropped low over the sorrel's neck, making himself as small a target as possible. There were two more shots but he didn't hear either of the slugs hit anything. The echoes faded and were swallowed up by the seeming infinity of the plain. But he stayed low on the sorrel's neck, trying to hold off panic, pawing sweat from his eyes so he could see where he was going.

Just ahead he spied what seemed to be an old Indian trail that wound away to the right, alongside a rock wall stained in autumnal yellows, reds, burnt umbers. He urged the panting horse onto the trail. Beyond the wall was a heaped mass of boulders; the path skirted them and then hooked back into a small, deeply eroded canyon. He glanced over his shoulder as he entered it, saw that he was hidden here from the posse. He straightened up in the saddle, letting his eyes roam the canyon walls. And felt his hopes plummet of a sudden, felt the fear pluck at him again.

The canyon was a box; the only entrance looked to be the one he'd just passed through.

He took the sorrel along the base of one of the sheer walls, frantically looking for a spot from which to make a stand. When he reached the far end he found one — a recess between a pair of large irregular boulders, half buried in a pocket of shadow, with the rocks overlapped in a way that offered plenty of cover. Dismounting, he led the sorrel behind the largest of the boulders. He was about to drop the reins when he realized that the cranny appeared to continue deeper into the canyon wall.

Another quick look satisfied him that the posse still hadn't discovered the canyon entrance. Entering the gap, he saw that it opened into a narrow tunnel or covered defile leading away into blackness. The faintest of drafts from within told him that there might be another opening — that the tunnel might lead all the way through the wall to emerge somewhere behind it.

The sorrel was still panting heavily from its long run, and when Glencannon led it into the passage it began to balk and make frightened snorting sounds. He caught hold of the horse's muzzle, stroked it until the animal gentled down. When it was quiet again he started forward, his right hand gripping the reins up close to the bridle.

They inched their way along the jagged face of

the rock scraping their bodies in the darkness. Rocks slipped and skittered beneath Glencannon's worn cowhide boots, beneath the sorrel's hooves. The entrance shrank behind them until it was little more than the glow of a kerosene lamp hung waist-high. The passage grew narrower, building a fear in him that the walls would press them into a cul-de-sac and trap them there.

But then the passage shifted sharply to the right, rising upward, and he saw another thin shaft of light fifty feet along. He took the sorrel toward it, watching the light grow to reveal an opening almost as wide as that in the canyon; only this one was in the ceiling of the tunnel, with the erosion of centuries having sifted gravel down to make a steep yet navigable path up to it. He maneuvered the tired horse up the grade and through the opening, into sunlight that burned against his eyes until they grew reaccustomed to its brilliance. Then he saw that he was standing on a small ledge on the opposite side of the canyon wall.

He turned to look back the way he had come. The tunnel had evidently been dug by nature to drain the sudden squalls and pounding winter rains from the cliff, perhaps one among dozens of similar defiles burrowed through the limestone. There was a good chance, he thought, that the men in the posse wouldn't know of this particular one, or be able to spot it unless they were as blind lucky as he'd been.

Laboriously, Glencannon climbed upward, leading the sorrel, until he reached the canyon's rim. There, he let his horse rest under an overhang of shale, made his way to a flat table rock and sank onto it. From that vantage point he could look down into the canyon below. Heat waves shimmered like translucent smoke; he shaded his eyes, blinking, licking parched lips.

The posse had just come into the canyon. He counted nine men, not eight as he'd previously thought. Sunlight reflected from the tarnished star on the chest of the lead rider, and even at this distance he recognized the man as Sheriff Oldham.

Oldham rode deeper into the box, the other men flanking him; just before they reached the wall on which Glencannon rested, the sheriff raised his hand to call a halt. They turned their horses in all directions, studying the shale and limestone cliffs, but none of them caught sight of the hidden passage. The sound of their horses' shod hooves on the bare rock floor drifted and echoed faintly throughout the confines of the box canyon.

At length Oldham and two of the other men dismounted and stood in a tight group. Glencannon could hear nothing of what was being said, but he sensed that it was an argument as to where their quarry might have gone. After a time, having reached some sort of decision, the three men remounted and Oldham motioned the posse around. There was some shouting and prancing about; then the riders fell into formation and threaded back out through the canyon's entrance.

Glencannon let out breath; they had apparently decided he hadn't entered this particular box after all, that he'd bypassed it for some other place of concealment. When they didn't find him, he thought, they'd give up the chase soon enough and head back to Wild Horse. The heat, the rough terrain, and the lack of water and food made that a certainty.

But it didn't mean he was out of harm's way. Far from it. The same problems faced him, lack of food and water being the worst of them; and there was also his wounded arm, his weakened condition and loss of blood. Unless he found shelter soon, a place where his wounds could be treated . . .

Painfully he straightened. On wobbly legs he returned to where the sorrel waited with lowered head in the shadows, caught up the reins, and led it back along the rim of the canyon.

It was near dusk when he found the waterhole.

He was some miles south of the box canyon by then. With unfamiliar trails and unknown landmarks, with several rest-stops to conserve what was left of his and the sorrel's strength, it had taken him all day to get this far. During those long, sun-blasted hours he had seen rattlesnakes and buzzards, endless stretches of primitive, rock-strewn landscape; but he hadn't seen any sign of a human or of human habitation, and he hadn't found anything to eat or drink.

The soles of his feet burned agonizingly, raw with blisters that had broken and bled. But still he walked most of the time, leading the horse. The sorrel was as weak as he was, and if it died in this desolation the last of his hopes would die with it. With the coming darkness, they could both rest and maybe recoup enough stamina to go on again tomorrow.

When he saw the line of straggly junipers far off to his left he thought at first that it was a mirage. His burning thirst drove him in that direction anyway, almost fatalistically. The junipers didn't vanish; they grew into sharper relief as he neared them. He realized then that they were real and that they marked the presence of moisture, perhaps a small creek or waterhole, and his fatalism gave way to a fresh surge of hope. He began to move faster, stumbling, half-dragging both himself and the horse.

The sun had begun to drop beyond the horizon before he finally staggered through a strain of sparse brown grass and reached the junipers. His head, his body, his wounded shoulder ached and throbbed with each step; the green and brown colors blurred in his vision. He plowed through the evergreens, pawed sweat from his eyes. And stood staring down at the waterhole.

It was dry.

Glencannon slumped to his knees, gasping.

The inside of his mouth and throat felt fiery, clogged with dust; his tongue seemed welded to the roof of his mouth. Thirst was an agonizing way to die. God, if only he had a few drops of water . . .

Half-delirious, he crawled into the middle of the sun-baked hole and began scooping at the earth with clawed fingers. The sun fell away behind the western buttes and the sky turned smoky, shot through with blood-red streaks. Glencannon paused several times in his frenzied labor, only to resume again after a few seconds. Then, at long last, the earth in the depression he'd made became damp. His digging turned feverish. Some two feet down, the first murky wetness began to seep through.

The sorrel nosed nearer, snuffling, drawn by the scent of water. Glencannon pushed it away and kept on digging until there was a small tepid puddle at the bottom. The horse shoved close again and its eyes were half-wild; Glencannon sank back and let it drink first. Then he widened the hole and leaned downward, immersing his face in the dark puddle, drinking greedily. The water was muddy and brackish and warm, but he'd never tasted better in his life.

When he'd drunk his fill he rested. After a time, he stripped off his shirt and probed the bullet wound in his shoulder. It had bled its last during the morning, but its blackened edges were rimmed with dirt and dried blood and it felt inflamed. Swaying a little, he washed his soiled kerchief and cleaned the wound as best he could. Exhaustion was creeping over him; his thoughts were sluggish and his eyes felt weighted, closing to slits. It wouldn't be long before he finally blacked out.

The low flat crack of a handgun shattered the early evening stillness, jerked him alert. The sorrel raised its head and nickered softly. Two more gunshots sounded; Glencannon's hand dropped automatically to the unfamiliar Remington holstered at his side, snapped it free.

More shots, three of them spaced a few seconds apart. His dulled senses finally registered that they were coming from some distance away and not directed at him. He listened, and when another volley sounded he pinpointed the location as a half-circle of sharp spires, like giant fenceposts, several hundred rods to the south; a few stunted trees grew there as well, blacker outlines against the purple-black sky.

Glencannon stood unsteadily, almost fell under a wave of dizziness. He caught the sorrel's reins, pulled the animal away from the waterhole and into the concealing shadows of the junipers. He knelt there, waiting, listening to several more shots echo through the darkness. A gun battle of some kind? Somebody target practicing at night? No way of knowing. The only thing for him to do was to stay where he was and keep quiet; couldn't afford to alert whoever it was doing that shooting over there.

But a feeling of heavy lethargy had started to

seep through him. The last of his strength ebbed away; he felt himself sagging forward, as if bone and muscle had somehow liquefied, and he was powerless to arrest the motion. Gritty dirt smacked against his cheek; he realized dimly that he had fallen on his side. He tried to rise but none of his limbs would respond. As if from a great distance, he heard the sorrel nicker again, then begin to whinny in a frightened way, as though a snake had appeared somewhere close by. His last thought was that whoever was among those spires yonder must have heard the sorrel, because now the shooting had stopped.

Then he lost his grip on consciousness and went spinning away into warm, empty black.

Nine

A swaying, jouncing motion brought him back to awareness. Pain stabbed through his shoulder, his head; there was something flat and hard underneath him. Mucus clung gluelike to the corners of his eyes, but he managed to pry them open and blink his vision clear. He was looking up at the dark night sky, at a three-quarter moon half-hidden by scudding clouds. His ears caught the familiar clatter of wagon wheels and springs bouncing over an uneven trail, and when he turned his head he could see the short wooden sides of a buckboard. He was lying inside the bed, his head pillowed by what felt like a bedroll and his lower body draped in a heavy woolen blanket.

He put the palms of his hands flat on the gapped boarding, raised himself slowly and painfully into a sitting position. Behind the wagon, he saw then, tied to it by a length of rope, was his sorrel; the horse moved in a tender stride but otherwise seemed fit. Glencannon ran a thick, cottony tongue over the roof of his mouth, started to twist around for a look at who was driving the buckboard. More pain sliced through his shoulder at the sudden movement, made the half-numbed fingers of his left hand prickle. He raised his good hand to touch the wound, found that it was crudely bandaged with something that felt like a strip of sackcloth. Then he eased around on his buttocks until he could look upward at the raised wagon seat.

A solitary figure sat there, a dark tensed outline in the pale moonlight. Who was he? Glencannon wondered groggily. Not the law; the man wouldn't be alone in a buckboard if he were. A neighborly citizen? But then what had all the shooting been about near the waterhole?

Glencannon blinked out at the surrounding terrain. They were still in the badlands; volcanic outcroppings, limestone spires and round-topped buttes loomed weirdly in each direction. The trail they were following was nothing more than a rutted cart track that could lead anywhere. Out to the prairie and back to Wild Horse? Glencannon wondered. Or south to Iron Bend? If the man up there intended to take him to one of the towns for doctoring, Glencannon would have to change his mind for him. He would stand no chance at all if the law got hold of him.

He slid his right hand down along his side, felt the leather of his shell belt and then the butt of the .44 Remington in his holster. So he hadn't been disarmed. He wrapped fingers around the scuffed wood, leaned forward to peer again at the buckboard's driver. Then he hesitated. Some of the cobwebs had gone out of his head, letting him think clearly again, and now the figure above seemed somehow familiar. As did the shaggy-rumped mare pulling the rig. Frowning, he moved again, trying to lift up onto his knees, and when he did that the heel of one boot cracked against the sideboard. The driver heard it; he swung his head around to look behind him. And in the slanting moonlight Glencannon recognized him.

Dale Brewer.

Relief rushed through him; he felt almost limp with it, and sank back onto one hip. "Dale," he said in a voice made hoarse by dust and strain. "By God, if you aren't the best sight I've seen in a long while!"

"Me too," the youth said. "How do you feel, Mr. Glencannon?"

Dale had always called him mister, even though Glencannon had insisted that the boy use his given name. But that was the way Dale was — polite, reserved in a positive sort of way. A good lad. Hell, a fine lad.

"Tired. And some weak."

"Maybe you'd best lie back down."

"No, I'll be all right. We headed for your ranch?"

"Yes, sir. It's about two miles from here."

"Your ma expecting us?"

"No. She doesn't know."

Glencannon licked at his cracked lips again. "You carrying a canteen, son? I could use some water."

"Yes, sir." Dale produced one from the seat

beside him, handed it down.

Glencannon drank. The warm water eased the dryness in his throat, took away some of the feeling of weakness that had settled through him. He said as he recapped the canteen, "You the one doing all the shooting I heard?"

Dale seemed to hesitate before he said, "Yes sir, that was me."

"How come?"

"I was practicing my aim."

"You usually do your practicing at night?"

"Sometimes. Pa . . . pa always said a man should learn how to shoot under any conditions, with a rifle and a handgun both."

"I reckon there's truth in that, all right," Glencannon said. "How'd you find me?"

"I heard your horse. He'd been spooked by a snake, I guess; he was pretty skittish when I came up."

"It's a lucky thing you picked that spot to do your practicing. I'd have likely died out there if you hadn't."

"Maybe not, Mr. Glencannon. I might have found you tomorrow too. I was fixing to go out looking for you, anyway."

"You mean you knew I was loose out here?"

"Yes, sir. I rode into town this morning; I wanted to talk to you about . . . well, about what you were going to do. I knew you wouldn't let Halacy and his Dollar Wagon bunch get away with what they did to pa."

"And you heard what happened last night."

Dale nodded. "I didn't believe it, though. You didn't kill Barber; I knew that."

"Was the posse back by then?"

"They came riding in while I was there. They said you'd given 'em the slip, but that you were wounded and you'd probably die out here. Sheriff Oldham telegraphed your description all over the Territory, just in case you didn't die."

"He's some lawman," Glencannon said bitterly.

"Yes, sir. Well, I rode out right away but it was still near dusk when I got back to the ranch. Ma said there was no sense trying to hunt for you in the dark —"

"Then she knows what happened in Wild Horse?"

"I told her first thing. And I talked her into letting me take the wagon out, just to look around for a bit and because she needed some juniper berries for an oil she makes."

Glencannon winced as one of the wheels jarred over a rock in the trail bed. They were beginning to descend now, and ahead he could see that the terrain gradually smoothed out into a long slope. At the foot of the slope, prairieland stretched away into the darkness. And off to the left edge of the flat, lamplight glowed in one of three lumpish black ranch buildings.

"It won't be long now," Dale said. "Why don't you just lie back and rest, Mr. Glencannon?"

"Reckon I will. But one more question first.

Were Halacy and his Dollar Wagon still in Wild Horse?"

"They were," Dale said thinly. "And fixing to stay another night before pulling up stakes."

"Do you know where they're headed next?"

"Word is Iron Bend."

Two-day ride from Wild Horse to Iron Bend, Glencannon thought as he lay back and re-pillowed his head on the bedroll. Maybe three with a big loaded wagon like theirs. If he was well enough to ride by tomorrow afternoon, there was a good chance he could catch up to Halacy before he reached Iron Bend, while the Dollar Wagon was camped somewhere along the road. He wasn't sure what he'd do then; that would take some thinking on. But he'd do something — whatever was necessary to avenge Clay Brewer's murder and clear his own name with Sheriff Oldham and the rest of the territorial law force.

It was another twenty minutes before they reached the ranch. Glencannon sat up again as Dale turned the mare through a splitrail fence gate and along a dusty path. The ranch house was made of weatherbeaten wood and mortared stone, as was a sagging barn off to one side; the third building was a square wooden box set adjacent to the corral, which Glencannon judged to be a combination tack room and storage shed. There was a well and a small windmill along one side of the house and a privy, a chicken coop, and a rabbit hutch spread out on the other. What looked to be a vegetable garden had been planted to the left of the access path.

The moonlight and darkness softened everything, but Glencannon knew that in the harsh light of day the place would look just like what it was: a hardscrabble ranch on a poor section of land. The best grazing land was to the west of Wild Horse, between it and Sawyer, but that was all controlled by large ranchers and Eastern cattle companies. The companies had had a hold on the area for some time, ever since Custer's expedition had confirmed gold in the badlands in 1874; they had brought in herds to feed the miners who flocked here in search of wealth, and who had eventually dubbed the fifty-mile stretch of rough country Gold Buttes. Newcomers to the area, like Clay Brewer, had had to settle for prairie land like this, sometimes sight unseen, misled as to its worth. It was not surprising that Brewer had lost some of his ambition after a time spent out here.

And yet Laurie had withstood the erosion of will, and so had Dale; they were special people, with a special strength. Clay had been a good man, but he had not even begun to realize how lucky he really was to have a wife like Laurie and a son like Dale. If he had, he wouldn't have treated either of them as he had during the past year.

Dale eased the mare to a stop between the house and the barn. As he did so the front door of the house opened and Laurie came out, standing outlined in a wedge of lamplight to peer across the yard. Then she saw the sorrel tied to the rear of the buckboard, and Glencannon rising up out of the bed, and she ran down off the porch and across the dusty earth, skirts flying.

"Jim!" she cried. "Jim!"

"He's all right, ma," Dale said. He had jumped down off the seat and come around to help Glencannon off. "I found him out by the dry waterhole near the Devil's Fenceposts."

She came to a halt in front of Glencannon, and for a moment it seemed to him that she wanted to fling her arms around him. "Thank God you're safe," she said, her voice thick with relief. "I've been worried sick ever since Dale came back from town."

"There were times today I didn't think I'd make it," he admitted. "Lord didn't figure it was my time, I guess."

Her gaze settled on his blood-caked shirt. "You're badly hurt, Jim! All that blood . . ."

"It's not as bad as it looks."

"We'll see about that. Dale, help me get him inside."

"I can walk all right," Glencannon said.

"Take his arm, son. Careful of the wound."

They led him across toward the house, and after half a dozen steps he was grateful for their support; his legs were still wobbly. Inside was a large main room — kitchen, dining room, parlor combined. A pair of closed doors in the far wall would lead to Dale's bedroom and to the one Laurie had shared with Clay. They helped him to one of the rough-hewn chairs at the table. There was an unlit lantern nearby — the light in the room came from a pair of wall lamps — and Laurie raised the glass, struck a sulphur match, and lit the wick.

"Fetch some water from the well," she said to Dale. "I'll bring medicine and bandages."

"Yes, ma."

Dale went out and Laurie disappeared through the nearest of the two bedroom doors. Glencannon sat slumped against the table, glancing around the room. It was sparsely furnished, though neat and well-scrubbed; the table, four chairs, an old mohair sofa, and a homemade rocker was all there was. An unpainted pineboard bookshelf stood against one wall, filled with books; Glencannon could make out the names of Shakespeare, Hawthorne, Fenimore Cooper. These, he knew, had once belonged to Laurie's father, Jeb Overholt, who had given them to Dale when he learned that the boy was an avid reader. The book spines, together with the chintz curtains that covered the windows and several stitched Bible quotations on the walls, lent color to the otherwise plain room.

The whole of the wall facing him was comprised of a massive stone-and-mortar fireplace, its hearth scorched black from countless fires built and carefully tended to ward off the freezing cold of Dakota winters. Some of the cooking was done in there, as a blackened kettle suspended from a spit rod testified. And the rest would be done on the small iron stove behind him, where a clay pot now simmered. The pungent odor of jackrabbit stew made Glencannon's stomach gnaw with hunger.

He felt the need for a smoke as well as for food. With his good hand he probed at his buttoned shirt pocket, found that he still had the makings, and brought them out. Holding the sack of Bull Durham in his teeth, by its drawstring, he creased one of the wheatstraw papers with thumb and forefinger. But he had difficulty with his left hand — the fingers were still half-numb — and he couldn't seem to get the sack open. He was fumbling with it when Laurie returned from the bedroom, carrying bandages and sulphur powder and a jar of some sort of salve.

"Here," she said, putting everything down on the table, "let me do that for you."

Glencannon smiled wanly. "Thanks."

Laurie opened the pouch, tapped tobacco from it into the V'd wheat-straw. As Glencannon was rolling it into a cylinder and licking the edge, Dale came in with a pan of fresh water. The youth stood watching as his mother scratched a match and lit Glencannon's cigarette.

"Go on out and tend to the horses," she said to him. "See that Jim's is rubbed down and fed."

"Can't I stay here awhile?" Dale asked. It was plain he was curious about what she and Glencannon might have to say to each other.

"No. Go on along now. There'll be supper when you finish."

Reluctantly, Dale obeyed. When he was gone Laurie stripped away Glencannon's blood-soaked shirt and studied the wound, biting her lip. Then she swabbed away the first and caked blood in gentle strokes, and some of the concern in her eyes eased.

"It doesn't look serious, Jim," she said. "The bullet went through cleanly. We'll have to be careful of infection, but you should be fine after two or three days in bed."

"I can't stay in bed two or three days," he said.

"Why can't you? You'll be safe here. The sheriff —"

"It's not the sheriff I'm worried about."

"You're not thinking of going after Halacy and his men?"

"That's just what I'm thinking. It's the only way I can clear my name. I don't want to be on the dodge for the rest of my life, Laurie."

"But —"

"Dale says they figure to leave Wild Horse for Iron Bend tonight or tomorrow; that'll put them on the trail for about three days — two nights camping. If I leave here tomorrow I should be able to catch up to them before they get to Iron Bend."

"Couldn't you wait until after they leave Iron Bend?"

"No. The more time goes by, the worse my chances of getting to them at all. Or of proving that they're the ones who killed Clay and the kid, Barber."

Laurie was silent for a time, applying sulphur powder to his wound and then spreading salve over it and tying bandages. At length she said, "What will you do when you catch up to them?" She seemed to have grudgingly accepted his position, despite evident misgivings; as long as he'd known her she'd been supportive as well as strong-willed. But the worry was still plain in her voice.

"I'm not sure yet," Glencannon answered. "I'll cross that bridge when I come to it. But there's got to be a way to handle it right. Halacy won't get away with what he did; I'll see to that, one way or another."

She finished bandaging his shoulder and stepped back. "I won't try to talk you out of leaving tomorrow, Jim," she said. "That's your decision. But tonight the decision-making is mine. I want you to go to bed and rest — no arguments."

He managed another wan smile. "No arguments. I sure could use a cup of coffee and a plate of that jackrabbit stew first, though."

"Lord, I forgot how hungry you must be! All right, a quick supper and then off to bed. You'll sleep in Dale's room. He can take the sofa out here."

She busied herself with plates and utensils and stove pots. Glencannon sat watching her, his arms resting on the table; his eyes felt gritty and

116

he could feel lethargy stealing over him again. Laurie was right: he needed a good night's rest, and then some, if he expected to do any long riding tomorrow.

When supper was on the table Laurie went out to the porch to call Dale. The boy came in a short while later and had little to say to either his mother or Glencannon. He ate with his head down and his eyes fixed on his plate, as if he had something weighing on his mind. Glencannon suspected it was Halacy and the Dollar Wagon bunch, but he was too exhausted to pursue the matter.

As soon as he finished eating he allowed Laurie to take his arm and lead him into Dale's bedroom. She pushed him down gently on the bed, removed his boots for him, and eased him back until his head lay cradled in the cool softness of a feather pillow. Then she covered him with a patchwork quilt, stood looking down at him for a long moment before moving out of the room. Glencannon was asleep almost instantly.

He slept deep and hard, and then dreamed that somebody was calling his name in an urgent voice, saying it over and over somewhere above him. He felt himself swimming up toward consciousness. But the voice wouldn't go away; it kept on saying, "Jim! Jim, wake up! Please, Jim!" Then sleep fell away from him and he was blinking up at Laurie bending over him, seeing her outlined against pink-gray dawn light that brightened the window behind her.

117

Her face was pinched with a mixture of consternation and fear, he realized, and he said immediately, "What is it, Laurie? What's the matter?"

"It's Dale," she said. "He's gone."

"Gone?"

"I've just been out to the barn. His horse is gone too. And so is the old cap-and-ball Colt Clay gave him on his fifteenth birthday. Oh God, Jim, I'm afraid he's decided to go after Halacy and the Dollar Wagon bunch himself!"

Ten

Glencannon struggled into a sitting position, pawing at his beard-stubbled face. His whole body felt stiff and sore, but the weakness of the night before seemed to have fled. Most of the pain was gone from his shoulder, too, and when he flexed the fingers of his left hand there was no numbness or prickling sensation. But he understood without thinking on it that it would be some time before he would be able to use that arm properly.

"Take it easy now," he said to Laurie. "Maybe the boy's just gone out riding somewhere, or into town —"

"No. He left before dawn and he didn't tell me he was going or leave me a note; those are two things he never does."

"But you don't know for sure that he's going after Halacy."

"Where else would he go? Jim, he's been moody ever since Clay's funeral. I've been worried about him; you could almost see things building up inside him, festering. And he doesn't know that you plan to go after Halacy yourself today — neither of us thought to tell him."

Glencannon scowled. He knew that Laurie

119

must be right; it would explain Dale's after-dark target practicing last night. The boy must be expecting Glencannon to spend a few days in bed, then to maybe ride out of the Territory to escape the law instead of chasing after Halacy and his bunch. It was just like a sixteen-year-old to figure he was the only one who could set matters right, and to rush off hell-bent for vengeance.

He said, "How long ago do you reckon he left?"

"I'm not sure. More than two hours, at least."

"Then I'd best get moving." He swung his legs out from under the quilt, eased himself onto his feet.

"You're going after him?" Laurie said.

"You know I am. I might not be able to catch up to him, considering he knows the trails better than I do, but I might get to the Dollar Wagon before he does anything foolish."

Some of the concern in her eyes transferred to him. "Are you sure you're well enough to ride?"

"I'm well enough."

"Jim . . ." she began, and then stopped. She stood only a few inches from him, her face upturned, and all at once he was aware of her nearness, of the scent of her and of his own near-nakedness. He felt stirrings deep inside, a rushing gather of heat that melted the reserve he'd always kept between them. Laurie seemed to feel it too; her breath quickened. Their eyes locked and hers had a smoky, yearning look that was half appeal and half sensual need. She made a soft sound in her throat and said his name again, this time in a different way. "Jim . . ."

Then she was in his arms, her body pressed against his, her lips open and moist, her fingers moving up along his bare back to the nape of his neck. The feel of her melted the last of his reserve; his mouth closed against hers, found it sweet and hot at the same time. The kiss seared him and he wanted to hold it, hold Laurie tight against him and lose himself in her warmth and softness.

And yet he couldn't. Guilt reared up inside him; he pulled his head aside, loosened his arms. But when her body slackened, too, and she cradled her face against his chest, he didn't push her away. He couldn't bring himself to break the contact of their bodies, not just yet.

"It's been so long," she said shakily. "So long . . ."

"Not this way, Laurie. It's not right this way."

"I know. But it could be right later, couldn't it?"

"Maybe. Laurie, I . . ."

"Don't say anything more, not now. There'll be time for it, Jim. Later." She drew back, looking up at him. "I'll get you some of Clay's things to wear. They should fit you. And some coffee; you'll want coffee."

Clay, he thought. *Clay's been dead not much more'n two days, and in the ground a day and a half. What the hell right have I got to be making love*

121

to his widow? His eyes slid away from Laurie's face; his hand came up and rubbed angrily, almost viciously, at his missing ear. Then he moved past her to the bureau near the window, began to pour water from the pitcher there into a tin washbasin.

Laurie watched him for a few seconds; he could feel her eyes on his back. Finally she left the room, but even when she was gone, the scent of her lingered. And her image lingered in his mind.

Laurie Overholt Brewer . . .

He had believed himself free of any feelings he might once have had for her. His few brief visits had been no match for all the long months apart from her; she had become, safely, a close friend and nothing more. Then why had he been attracted to her again in Wild Horse, and overwhelmed just now by that swift upsurge of passion? He couldn't explain it — he was afraid to try — and yet he couldn't deny the truth of it. And what of Laurie? Had her response to him been nothing more than the hunger of a woman long denied pleasures of the flesh? Or had it been an emotional impulse triggered by sorrow and fear for the safety of her son? Or, as her words had implied, did she really care for him after all — a man like him, a drifter with a missing ear and no goal in life?

"It could be right later, couldn't it? Don't say anything more, not now. There'll be time for it, Jim. Later . . ."

Glencannon shook himself, cursing, and forced his thoughts back to the urgent matters at hand. He had to keep a clear head; he couldn't afford to start brooding now, to give in to his emotions. The only way he could hope to help Dale, and to clear his name with Sheriff Oldham by facing down the Dollar Wagon outfit, was to keep his wits about him. Otherwise, and any way you looked at it, he was liable to wind up dead.

He finished washing his face and dried off on a towel racked nearby. Laurie came back in then with a pair of laundered Levi's and a folded cotton shirt, laid them on the bed. She didn't say anything to him, but she did give him a grave smile on her way out. She didn't seem embarrassed or ill at ease over what had just happened — and what had almost just happened — between them. Her thoughts, like his, seemed to have resettled on Dale.

There was coffee waiting when he finished dressing and came out into the main room. He said as he caught up the mug, "I'll need Clay's rifle, if it's here. And a pair of field glasses."

She nodded. "We've got both."

"You'll also have to give me an idea of the quickest route from here to the road between Wild Horse and Iron Bend."

"You won't need that now," she said. "I'm going with you, Jim."

He stared at her. "What put that notion in your head?"

"It's not a notion. Dale's my son and I'm not

going to sit around here alone, waiting for you to come back or somebody to bring me news of another death or two. Besides, I know the badlands better than you do; I can lead you to the road easier than I can direct you."

"Laurie . . ."

"I can handle a horse," she said resolutely, "and I can handle a gun. I'm not a helpless town woman, Jim. You ought to know that well enough."

"I know it."

"Well, then?"

Glencannon struggled with his feelings. He knew that everything she said was true, and yet he didn't want her with him. It would be dangerous, going after Halacy and his bunch; the thought of her getting hurt frightened him. There was another reason, too: he was afraid of being too close to her, afraid her nearness might distract him and he'd lose his head again and not be able to control his desire for her.

"I don't think you should come," he said.

Laurie went to the front window, stood there with her arms folded and stared out at the vastness beyond. "I'm going with you, Jim," she said, "and that's all there is to it. You can't stop me short of tying me to a chair."

"Damn it . . ."

She turned, her eyes meeting his levelly. "I'll pack some food and water while you get the horses ready. Clay's rifle and field glasses are in the bedroom; I'll fetch them out."

Before he could say anything she crossed to the bedroom, disappeared inside. Glencannon drank more of his coffee, still struggling with himself. But what was he going to do? She'd made up her mind and she could be mule-stubborn, he remembered, when she had her sights set on something. He had no right to order her to stay here, or to keep her here against her will. Dale was her son — and Clay had been her husband; she had every reason to do as she saw fit.

When she came out of the bedroom three minutes later she was carrying an old pair of field glasses, a .44-40 Winchester and a box of shells. She had also changed out of the dress she had been wearing, into a split corduroy riding skirt and a man's shirt. She handed rifle, glasses, and shells to Glencannon, saying, "Are we going to argue any more? Or are we going after Dale?"

He let breath hiss out between his teeth. "No more arguments," he said shortly. "I'll be in the barn." And he turned and went outside.

The sun had begun to climb up over the eastern horizon, turning the sky the color of an old copper pot. An early-morning wind blew hot against his face as he crossed the yard to the barn. It was going to be hotter today than yesterday, he judged, and tried not to think about what the heat would do to him in his weakened condition. It sapped a man's strength at the best of times; and a man with a bullet wound in his shoulder, and two days' worth of hard times just behind him, was hardly a match for it. He'd have to make sure to drink plenty of water before they left, and that they took at least two full canteens with them in case there were no waterholes or streams along the route they would travel. Some folks believed you should conserve water in the badlands, only wet your lips with it or take a few swallows at a time; but others, especially those who'd had dealings with plains or desert Indians, knew better. Saturate yourself with water and you'd keep your strength up a lot easier than the other way around.

Inside the barn Glencannon found his rested sorrel in one of three stalls. The second stall was empty and the third was occupied by the shaggy-rumped mare. Clay's horse had evidently not found its way home yet, assuming the tow-head, Barber, had turned it loose in Wild Horse; either that, or it had been stolen by someone along the way. He spent ten minutes saddling both animals — the .44-40 Winchester went into the scabbard along the sorrel's flank, the field glasses around the pommel. He used his left arm as little as possible, but by the time he was finished there was pain in his shoulder again and the muscles along his back were beginning to protest.

He led the horses out of the barn, over in front of the house. Laurie came out with a pair of canteens and a sack of food. Glencannon stowed the sack in the sorrel's saddlebags while Laurie draped one canteen around each saddlehorn.

"I'll want to take water before we go," he said.

She nodded. "I'd best doctor your shoulder again too; it'll only take a minute. I don't like the way you hold your arm."

"It's all right," he said.

"No more arguments, remember?"

She led him inside, and while he drank three dippersful of well water she changed his bandage, applying more of the sulphur powder and salve she'd used the night before. Then she made him take a chunk of salted beef jerky, took another for herself, to eat while they rode. The salt, too, would help fight off the dehydrating effects of the heat.

Wordlessly they went back outside and mounted up, Laurie sitting the mare like a man instead of perching sidesaddle as ladies usually rode. She was a woman to admire, he thought. Christ, but she was. How could Clay have treated her as he had? How could he have held off touching her, making love to her . . .

Glencannon shook himself again, got a tight rein on his emotions. No more of that, damn it. No more! He bit down hard on the chunk of jerky, gigged the sorrel into a trot. Laurie brought the mare up alongside him before he was halfway to the front gate.

Eleven

Instead of riding southwest across the prairie, as Glencannon might have expected, Laurie pointed them back along the trail he'd traveled with Dale the night before. The main wagon road between Wild Horse and Iron Bend, she told him, curled around until it cut through the badlands in a line due east, skirting the worst of the rough country and the ghost town called Gold Buttes. Following the badlands trails would bring them to the road a good six miles nearer Iron Bend than if they crossed the prairie and save them at least three hours' time. Dale knew this as well as she did, she said; she was convinced that this was the way he would have come.

They rode as fast as the terrain would allow, stopping now and then to let the horses blow in a shady place or to answer a nature call. Neither spoke much. There was little to say at this point, and the building heat took enough of their energy as it was.

Some past noon, the terrain grew rougher and the trail began to climb at a steep angle; jagged chunks of stone and shale were strewn around as if thrown indiscriminately by a giant hand. The horses started to labor again, forcing Laurie and

Glencannon to dismount and walk them upward. The midday heat was savage. Glencannon could feel it sucking moisture out of him, sapping his buildup of strength. Beside him, Laurie's breath came in irregular pants and he could see that her face was flushed and slick with sweat. But she hadn't complained, nor had she been the one to suggest a rest-stop at any time. He knew that she was determined to plunge onward until they reached the wagon road, and maybe determined to prove her worth to him as well.

When they topped the incline they came upon a small grotto hollowed out of a fan-shaped rock. Along one side was a kind of natural stone bench, shaded from the sun. Glencannon stopped and let the sorrel's reins fall.

"We'll rest here for a spell," he said.

Laurie seemed to want to protest, then nodded wearily and said, "All right, Jim."

He moved into the grotto first with the Remington drawn, checking for snakes that had crawled in out of the sun. There were none. Satisfied of that, he led the horses into the shade, unslung one of the canteens, and poured water into the crown of his hat. While the animals drank, Laurie unpacked the sack of food and opened it up on the stone bench.

They sat side by side, but not touching, and ate salted jerky and home-canned applesauce, washing it down with gulps of warm water. Neither of them said much at first, but Glencannon could feel Laurie's eyes on him. Once he glanced over at her; her gaze didn't waver. Thoughts of her attractiveness and desirability once more began to rag his mind and he felt uncomfortable again, angry at himself. He turned his head away, lifted one hand to brush at his missing ear.

Laurie said, "Why do you do that, Jim?"

"Do what?"

"Rub at the scar where your ear used to be. You do it all the time when you're around me."

He felt a cut of embarrassment. "That's not a fit topic for conversation," he said gruffly.

"Why isn't it? Jim, you don't have to be ashamed of that scar."

"What makes you think I'm ashamed of it?"

"But you are and we both know it. Do you think it matters to people — to me? Is that why you try to hide it by keeping your hair so long?"

"Damn it, it's a deformity —"

"Lots of people have deformities," Laurie said. "On the inside, as well as on the outside. The outside ones aren't important; the inside ones are. Like the one Clay had, for instance."

Glencannon had an impulse to get up, walk away from her and this conversation. Instead he pulled out the makings, started to build himself a shuck. "I don't think it's right to talk about Clay," he said.

"Jim, he's dead and buried. We can't change that. And you and I have to go on living, don't we?"

The smoke from his cigarette tasted hot and

raw; he stubbed it out after only two drags, hurled the butt past the horses into the blaze of sunlight.

"Jim?"

He still said nothing.

"All right," she said, and he heard her sigh. "I'm ready to ride again, if you are."

Glencannon shoved onto his feet, gathered up the canteen and the food and took them to the horses. By the time he swung into leather Laurie was already astride her mare and gigging it out of the grotto. When he caught up with her she looked at him once, almost forlornly, but she didn't speak. He felt the need to say something to her, yet no words came to him — or at least, no words that he could bring himself to say aloud.

They rode in silence again, through the heat of the afternoon. The jouncing movement of the sorrel made pain flare up in his wounded shoulder, as it had off and on during the morning; but it was tolerable, not much worse than that of a nagging toothache. He kept flexing the fingers of that left hand, to keep them and the arm from stiffening up. He was going to have enough trouble facing down Halacy and his three hard cases without doing it half-crippled.

The terrain smoothed out some after a time, the heavy scatter of boulders and rock formations thinning into parched, sun-hardened earth, patches of grama grass, and growths of juniper and stunted cottonwood. Past three o'clock they came on a place where the trail forked into two wider branches, one leading due south and the other veering off to the west, where high buttes and craggy hills loomed rust-colored against the burning sky. Both roads showed deep wheel ruts, the kind made by heavily laden ore wagons during the rainy season when the ground was soft and muddy.

Laurie drew rein first and pointed up the western branch. "That leads to the town of Gold Buttes," she said. "It used to be a thriving mining settlement, so I've been told, but now that the gold's gone nobody lives there anymore."

Glencannon nodded. He'd been there once, a dozen years back. "How far are we from the main wagon road?" he asked.

"Not far. An hour or so. We should be able to see it pretty soon."

They continued along the southern road. Some of the heat was beginning to fade out of the day and Glencannon was grateful for the respite; he could feel himself flagging again. Every part of his body felt sore and his arms were heavy with fatigue. He would have to rest when they came in sight of the Iron Bend road, take more water and more nourishment. There was no sense in trying to drive himself beyond his limits. He couldn't help Dale if he was half-dead and about to fall out of his saddle when he caught up with the Dollar Wagon.

It was four-thirty by Glencannon's stem-

132

winder when they topped a rise grown with black raspberry bushes and came in sight of the main road. The road still followed the shrunken line of the Wild Horse River here, and from this vantage point Glencannon could look down a long, gradual slope for a half-mile or so in three directions. There was nobody on the road, nobody on or near the river, that he could see with the naked eye.

He eased himself out of the saddle, looped the field glasses off the saddlehorn, and went to where a gnarled mulburry threw dappled shade over the ground. He sank down there and used the glasses to sweep the wagon road, the riverbank, the parched grassland beyond to the east. Nothing, no sign of the Dollar Wagon or of Dale or his roan horse.

Laurie had come to sit beside him. When he lowered the glasses she said, "Did you see anything, Jim?"

"No. The Dollar Wagon must have already passed this point."

"If they left Wild Horse this morning, that's not likely. They wouldn't be able to travel that fast with a loaded wagon."

"Then they're still back to the north somewhere?"

"I'd say so, yes."

"All right," Glencannon said. "But what about Dale? Would he be fool enough to go after them in the daylight?"

"Lord," she said reverently, "I hope not."

"Did he have a rifle or a shotgun of his own?"

"No. Just that old cap-and-ball pistol."

"Well, he's got to have some sense," Glencannon said, grim-voiced. "Only a duncehead would try to throw down on four men in broad daylight with a single-shot handgun." He paused, thinking. "Still, he must have back-trailed along the road, looking for them. Otherwise, he'd be somewhere around here."

"Maybe he is," Laurie said. "Mightn't he have hidden himself down there to wait for them?"

"If he did, he's found a right perfect spot."

"What should we do?"

"Nothing for a little while. Horses need rest and so do I." He looked up at the sky. "It'll be dusk in another hour or so. If Dale or the Wagon hasn't shown by then, I'll ride out looking."

He stood up again, mindful of the soreness in his body, and went back to unsheath the .44-40 Winchester from the sorrel's saddle scabbard. "Lead the horses over on the other side of the rise," he told Laurie, "and picket them out of sight of the trail. Doesn't seem this road is used much nowadays, but we don't want to take any chances."

"All right, Jim."

"We'll make camp yonder, beyond that mulberry. Rocks'll give us cover, but we'll still have a good look down below."

Laurie led the horses away. Glencannon made his way slowly to the jumble of rocks beyond the mulberry tree, found a cleared space where they wouldn't have to worry about snakes. He lowered himself onto a flat rock like a tree stump, propped his elbows on his knees, and scanned the main road and the line of the river again. Still deserted. Nothing moved anywhere, except for a hawk circling lazily in the heat-smoked sky and a prairie chicken scurrying among the rocks off to one side.

When Laurie came back she was carrying one of the canteens and the food sack. She handed Glencannon the canteen, saying, "The other one's empty. This is all the water we've got left."

He shook it. Less than half full. "I can fill up at the river tonight," he said. He took a drink, passed the canteen back to Laurie, shook his head when she offered him another piece of jerked beef. Then he slid down off the rock, laid his back against it and tipped his hat down low, on his forehead to shade his eyes.

Minutes passed in silence. Laurie made restless stirring sounds nearby, finally came over to sit beside him. Her shoulder touched his; he was instantly conscious of the warmth and softness of her body, the sweat-spiced woman smell of her. In spite of himself, fantasy images flickered across his mind and there was the faint ache of desire in his loins. He moved away from her, sliding his shoulders along the rock.

She didn't try to come close to him again. But after a few seconds she said, "Talk to me, Jim. I can't stand this silence; it's so still out here, it makes me think of the graveyard where we buried Clay."

"Talk about what?"

"Anything. About yourself. What have you done since we last saw you? Where have you been?"

"You don't want to hear about that."

"But I do. Tell me."

Her voice was almost pleading, and when he looked at her he realized that beneath her external calm, she was desperately worried and frightened about Dale. A wave of tenderness overtook him. He wanted to reach out, hold her in his arms again as he had at the ranch, comfort her; he wanted to make things right for her, take away the hurt and put the smile he remembered so well back on her lips. But he could do none of those things, not now, not yet. All he could do was give her the words about himself that she had asked for.

He began to talk. He told her about the months riding fence in Wyoming, the freight-hauling job in Montana, the cowpunching in Colorado and for King Rowan this past summer. He told her some of the things he had seen and done, and what a drifter's life was like. She didn't interrupt. She didn't say anything at all until he was finished and starting to roll himself a cigarette.

"What about women, Jim?" she asked then.

"Women?"

"You're not a monk. You've known women, surely."

"A few. But you don't want to hear about them."

"Saloon girls?"

"That kind, yes."

"No other kind? No respectable women?"

"No."

"Why? Because of your missing ear?"

"Laurie, let's not start that up again —"

"I just want to know why you never married, that's all."

"Because I never found the right woman."

"Is that the only reason?"

"Yes, it's —"

He broke off. Down on the road, a lone rider had come into view from the north, moving at a leisurely gait. Glencannon scooped up the field glasses, fitted them against his eyes, focused on the rider. But the man was a stranger — an ordinary cowhand, from the looks of him. He lowered the glasses again.

Laurie said tensely, "That isn't Dale — ?"

"No. A stranger." Glencannon stirred, pulled himself to his feet. The lower rim of the sun had slid down behind the hills and buttes to the west; the sky was flame-streaked in that direction. It was still a half-hour before dusk, but he was conscious of a restlessness inside him now, a renewed need for activity. "Not much point in waiting any longer," he said. "Wagon may still come along, but Halacy might also have camped somewhere uptrail for the night. I'd best get moving."

"I'm going with you," Laurie said.

"No, you're not. Not this time. Nightstalking is a man's business. Besides, I'll have enough to worry about without adding you to the list."

She bit her lower lip. "I suppose you're right," she said. "But are you sure you're well enough to ride alone?"

"I'm well enough," Glencannon told her. There was some lie in that — he still felt weak and his shoulder pained him — but not enough to make the words unreasonable.

"You'd better let me check your wound —"

"No, never mind. It hasn't been bleeding." He bent for the rifle and the field glasses. "You stay here and keep out of sight. I'll leave you my handgun for protection."

"I don't need it, Jim."

"You'll take it anyway, just in case. I won't need more than the Winchester."

Laurie went with him to the horses, where he sheathed the rifle on the sorrel's flank and then handed her the Remington from his holster. "I'll try to be back before morning," he said. "But if I'm not here by sunup, you fill up that other canteen at the river and head back to your ranch. Don't be waiting around here."

She nodded. The fear and anxiety glistened in her eyes as she looked up at him.

"Try not to worry, Laurie," he said softly. "I'll bring Dale back to you, safe and sound."

She looked at him a moment longer, and there was something else in her eyes, some other emotion. Then she came forward, put her arms around him, pressed herself close, and found his mouth with hers, a brief dry kiss. He had no time to react; the pressure of her body was gone and she had stepped back almost immediately.

"Bring yourself back to me too, Jim," she said. "Safe and sound."

Twelve

The sun had disappeared to the west, turning the buttes and hills into black shapes that looked pasted against the sky's fading sunset colors, when Glencannon reached the main wagon road. He paused there to use the glasses while there was still daylight; the road remained deserted in both directions, and there were no sights of smoke from a campfire. He gigged the sorrel to the north, riding on the side of the road nearest the river, his eyes restless and watchful for any movement among the nearby rocks and trees.

Twilight was brief; it faded out of the sky like dye out of an old shirt. Night shadows formed rapidly, and a three-quarter moon and a dazzle of stars softened the purple-black through which Glencannon rode. On the sections of the river that he could see, the pale moonlight reflected thin silver images off its muddy surface.

The tension in him grew, even though the road ahead and behind stayed empty. If Laurie had been right and the Dollar Wagon was still somewhere in this direction, then Halacy and his men had to be close by now. That is, *if* they'd left Wild Horse this morning as they'd been intending to. It would make matters a hell of a lot worse if they hadn't, he thought grimly. He wasn't in any shape to ride all the way to Wild Horse tonight; and even if he was forced to try it, by the time he got there Dale might already have done something foolish and 'disappeared' the same way his father had . . .

Agitatedly Glencannon reached down and slid the Winchester part way out of the saddle scabbard, so he could clear it in a hurry if the need arose. He wanted a smoke but begrudged the time it would take to stop and build one. He settled instead for another drink from the almost empty canteen.

The road had begun to rise sharply here, winding upward along a low bluff. There was another bluff on the opposite side of the river, forming a gorge through which the waterway ran. Glencannon took the sorrel up the incline at a slow trot, conserving the animal's strength.

He was nearing the place where the road crested along the rim when he saw the smoke.

It crept skyward in thin wisps from a section of the river hidden by the bluff. He jerked back on the reins, bringing the horse up short. Lifting his lean body in the saddle, he peered up at the smoke and satisfied himself it was the kind that came from a campfire. He guided the sorrel off the road and across rough, bare ground toward the edge of the bluff. When he neared it he dismounted, dropped the reins, and stroked the animal's forehead to keep it quiet. Then he crept forward to the edge, dropped prone, peered down along the steep slope, upriver.

The Dollar Wagon was there, pulled off a secondary track that would have its beginnings somewhere farther along the main road. There was a screen of trees on the far side of the wagon, bordering the track; their horses were picketed near here. The campfire had been built on the side facing toward Glencannon, and in its ruddy glow he could make out four figures — two of them moving around, the other two hunkered near the fire. As he watched, one of the moving figures went down to the river, maybe thirty rods from the wagon, and fetched up a coffee pot of water.

Glencannon shifted position on the rough ground, then eased back away from the edge. He returned to the sorrel, slid the Winchester the rest of the way out of the scabbard and caught up the field glasses. Then he led the animal some ways back toward the road, looped its reins around a branch on the decaying trunk of a cedar; now if the horse made a sound, it was not likely to carry all the way down to where Halacy and the others were.

Back on his belly again at the bluff's lip, Glencannon raised the glasses to his eyes and used the campfire to focus them as best he could. There was enough light from there and from the pale moon to give him a fair look at what was going on around the wagon, but the shadows were too thick in the trees and back up the secondary trail to make out much. If Dale was somewhere in that vicinity, he couldn't locate him from here.

He moved forward a little and swept a look over the slope. It was heavily grown with sagebrush and with blackberry and gooseberry bushes; the shadows were thick there, too, and nothing moved among them. Dale could be here just as well as he could be among the trees. Or he could be across the river, at the base of the other bluff, where there was a scatter of rocks and more trees; the river was narrow at this point and looked shallow enough to wade. Or he could be nowhere near here — but that was a hope Glencannon wasn't prepared to put stock in.

Nor did he want to put stock in the one other possibility: that Dale had already made his play against Halacy, long before this, and been given a bullet and a shallow grave for his daunciness.

There was nothing to do now, he thought, but wait. Not much was likely to happen while the men down there were up and moving about. The time to make a move was after they were all asleep; even a headstrong boy would realize that. But the prospect of waiting hours up here in the darkness didn't bother Glencannon. Now that he'd found the Dollar Wagon, the restlessness had gone out of him and the tension was no longer urgent. A lot of years and too many brushes with trouble had taught him patience, among other lessons, when the situation called for it.

He crawled a few feet to his left, being Indian

quiet about it, to where a patch of dry grass cushioned the hard ground and there was a small cutaway in the bluff's edge. The cutaway gave him a better shooting angle if he needed to use the Winchester. He settled onto the grass, favoring his left side because of the dull-pain in his shoulder. And he waited.

The four men below cooked and ate a meal; the smell of frying meat and boiling coffee floated up to Glencannon on the still air and made his stomach muscles clench. Then they sat around the fire for a time, smoking, probably jawing with each other, the burning ends of their cigarettes and seegars winking like fireflies in the pale dark. Then two of them stood and went to pitch the wedge tents, and after three or four minutes a third began to lay out a bedroll. The one still relaxing around the fire, Glencannon judged, was Jersey Jack Halacy. He looked content down there, a man enjoying an after-supper smoke with nothing troubling his mind or his conscience. The cold-blooded murder of at least two men and probably more over the years didn't seem to bother him one whit. Or men like him. Glencannon had never understood that kind of man. He had too much respect for human life himself, and the men he'd been forced to kill — two, both in self-defense — still haunted his sleep of a night now and then.

But there were a lot of Jersey Jack Halacys roaming the western frontier, particularly in the territories that hadn't yet been granted statehood, and until the laws became firmer, the lawmen better organized and better qualified than ones like Harrison Oldham, the outlaws and con men and grifters would continue to flourish. And maybe not even then, Glencannon thought wryly. Maybe there would always be Jersey Jack Halacys, even in the days when law and order finally prevailed, to prey on the weak and the gullible and the foolish.

When the tents were up one of the men turned in right away — it looked to be the monte dealer, the one called Jess. Halacy and the other two had another smoke together at the fire. Ten minutes later, Halacy stood and took a slow stroll down by the river; the other two crawled into their bedrolls. And after another ten minutes, Halacy came back, stood looking around at the wagon and the campsite like a satisfied monarch surveying his little kingdom, and then disappeared inside the other tent.

Glencannon shifted his cramped body into a more comfortable position; lifted the glasses and scanned the trees beyond the wagon, the base of the bluff across the river, the slope below him. Nothing moved anywhere. One of the horses near the wagon made a nervous neighing sound; Glencannon's sorrel made a soft answering nicker and then was still. A screech owl made its peculiar cry somewhere in the distance. Otherwise the night was hushed.

The campfire banked; the embers began to lose some of their ruddy glow. Neither of the two men stirred in their bedrolls nearby. Glencannon fished out his stem-winder, flipped the lids, and held the face up at an angle to the moon. It was after ten o'clock. He put the watch away, rolled over on his belly again. Come on, boy, he thought. If you're out there, come ahead and make your move.

Stillness.

Glencannon could feel his eyelids growing heavy. He hadn't had much rest in the past few days and the fatigue was beginning to tell on him. He was already having to fight off the warm lassitude that preceded sleep; he couldn't fight it off all night long. Another hour or two or three and he would —

Something moved over on the secondary trail, beyond the wagon.

Instantly Glencannon was alert. He raised up on his forearms, his right hand dragging the Winchester over in front of him. The movement came again, a shadow-shape detaching itself from the heavier shadows of the cottonwoods, starting to come downward at the edge of the track. Glencannon hauled up the glasses, peered through them at the shape making its stealthy way toward the wagon. It looked like Dale, all right. He couldn't be sure in the darkness, but the size was right and there was something in the figure's hand that had to be a gun.

His first feeling was one of relief: the boy was still alive and unharmed. But then the relief gave way to a new sense of urgency. The next few minutes were going to determine whether or not Dale *stayed* alive and unharmed. And it was all up to him to see to it that he did.

Putting the glasses down, Glencannon butted the Winchester against his right shoulder and sighted along the barrel. The boy came down out of the shadows, into the open space between the trees and the wagon. There he paused, looking over toward the two sleeping men in the bedrolls; then he eased forward again, at an angle that would let him skirt the rear of the wagon to the nearest wedge tent, the one in which Halacy slept.

One of the picketed horses stirred and made a sound that carried up to where Glencannon was. Dale froze. Both men by the fire moved under their blankets but neither of them woke. A full minute passed before Dale moved again, took three hesitant strides that brought him to the rear corner of the wagon.

Glencannon squeezed off and put a bullet into the wagon's gaudily painted side, three feet from where the boy was.

The sound of the shot sent ringing echoes bouncing between the walls of the two bluffs. Dale leaped back, looking around in wild confusion. The two by the fire sat up groggily, the way men do when they've been wrenched out of a heavy sleep. Glencannon fired again, and then again; both bullets kicked up dirt and sod sprang in front of the terrified youth. And he did what Glencannon had intended him to do.

Dale spun on his heels and ran for the trees.

Halacy had come crawling out of his tent, gun in hand. So had the monte dealer, Jess. The other two were on their feet now, looking around in the same wild confusion as Dale had seconds ago, trying to pinpoint the location of the shots. Glencannon let them see where he was; he fired three more times in succession, spraying bullets into the campfire — sparks and embers flew — and into the ground between Halacy and Jess. All four men scrambled for cover, Halacy diving for one corner of the Dollar Wagon, Jess for the other corner, the remaining two for the bushes that grew along the bluff's base.

Dale had already disappeared into the trees. Glencannon couldn't tell whether or not the boy had been seen; but Halacy and the other three were directing their attention to the bluff in front and above them, not to the cottonwoods behind them, and that was a good sign. Guns opened up from behind the wagon and the berry bushes. But they were using handguns, not rifles, and none of the shots came close. The sound of the shooting created a hammering din in the darkness; the picketed horses began kicking at their tethers, neighing with fright.

Glencannon had stuffed a handful of cartridges into his pocket earlier; he reloaded quickly, put two more shots into the Dollar Wagon and two more after that toward the muzzle flashes below. That would keep them pinned down for awhile, make them think twice before they rushed around to saddle their horses and mount a chase. Then he shoved back from the cutaway, dragging the rifle and the field glasses, and hoisted himself to his feet. He ran in a low crouch to where the sorrel was tied. The animal's ears were pricked up and it was pawing the ground nervously, but it didn't shy away from him as he looped the glasses over the saddlehorn and jammed the Winchester into the scabbard.

He swung into leather. They were still shooting down below; the echoes kept rolling and bouncing between the bluff walls. He heeled the sorrel around, took it at an angle toward the road. When he got there he was only a few rods from the crest, and he thought he could hear the pounding of hooves approaching on the other side. Dale? He ran the sorrel up to where he could look along the flat crest and the incline on the far side.

A horse and rider were coming up that incline at full gallop, away from the place below where the secondary track intersected the main road. The rider had his head down and didn't see Glencannon coming toward him until he was up on the flat; then when he did he was so startled that he jerked back hard on the reins, made his horse rear and almost pitch him. There were no more than ten rods separating them when that happened, and there was no question then that the rider was young Dale Brewer.

"It's me, boy!" Glencannon yelled at him.

"Jim Glencannon!"

Dale had his roan under control again, and for a second Glencannon thought he hadn't heard the shout and was going to bolt away in the direction he'd just come. But then the sense of the words seemed to penetrate, and he recognized Glencannon; he heeled forward as Glencannon neck-reined the sorrel around and came up beside him.

"It was *you*," Dale said in amazement. He sounded frightened and looked it too, white face shining in the moonlight. "You were the one who shot at me."

"To save your damn-fool hide," Glencannon snapped at him. The shooting had stopped now; he could hear the faint sound of men yelling at each other on the far side of the bluff. "Never mind the talking now; we haven't got much time. Ride, boy. Ride!"

He dug his bootheels into the sorrel's flanks. Moments later Dale was beside him. And they sent their horses plunging hell-bent along the road to the south.

Thirteen

They rode hard for the better part of half an hour, sending up thick plumes of dust that hung in the hot dry air behind them like signal smoke. Glencannon kept swinging his head around to see if they were being pursued, but he couldn't see anything through the dust. He thought that Halacy and his bunch would be back there; no man likes to be shot at in the middle of the night, particularly by an unknown rifleman, and Halacy's kind would like it even less. Back-shooters and outlaws never liked to be given a dose of their own medicine. They'd be giving chase, all right. And maybe, just maybe it would work out for the best that way.

When they neared the place where the rutted trail to Gold Buttes intersected the main road, Glencannon raised up in the saddle and gestured to Dale to slow up. They slackened speed to a fast trot. Then Glencannon pointed off toward the buttes, veered his horse off the road in that direction. The sloping ground was covered with dry grass and littered with rocks; the rough going made him, and Dale behind him, slow his pace even more. But their horses' hooves no longer spun up billows of dust, and it was less than four hundred yards on a diagonal course to where the

Gold Buttes trail crested the first rise and Laurie was hidden with her mare.

Halfway upward across the rocky ground Glencannon threw another look over his shoulder. The dustclouds along the road had begun to settle; he could see most of the way back to where the road hooked eastward, following the river. There was still no sign of Halacy and his hirelings. But they couldn't be far behind, he knew, and it would only be a matter of minutes before they came pounding into sight. He and Dale would have to have reached the cover of the rocks above by then or they would be clearly outlined in the moonlight.

The sorrel's muscles heaved under him as it fought its way upward; he could hear its snorting, labored breath and the ringing of its shoes against rock. There was no use in trying to urge more speed out of the animal, not on terrain like this, where one false step could mean a broken leg.

Dale drew abreast as another hundred yards fell away behind. Glencannon didn't look at him: instead he peered toward the black shape of the mulberry tree, visible now in silhouette against the sky. Laurie had to know they were coming by this time, but she wouldn't show herself until she recognized them.

With maybe a hundred yards to go, he glanced once more over his shoulder. The main road was still empty. Going to make it, he thought, and a kind of grim elation swept over him. He knew what his next order of business would be, and it wasn't to hide in the rocks or head deeper into the bad lands. Now that Dale was safe, the lethargy had left him and the tension had hardened into cold purpose. He was through running away, and through taking the kind of defensive action he had back at Halacy's encampment. The time had come to bite the bullet; he wasn't going to have a much better chance to clear himself with the law and put Halacy and his bunch behind bars where they belonged.

The rutted wagon trail loomed ahead. As soon as the laboring horses pulled them onto it, Laurie came out from behind the nearby rocks and raced toward them. Both Glencannon and Dale drew sharp rein, swung down without letting go of the leads. Far back to the north, dust was just starting to boil up on the main road: less than five minutes remained before the outlaws would ride close enough to see this far up the slope.

Laurie reached them, crying, "Dale!" and threw her arms around the boy. "Oh, thank God you're all right!"

Glencannon said, "We've got to get the horses out of sight." The tone of his voice made it a command.

He pulled the panting sorrel uptrail and over on the far side of the rise, to where Laurie had picketed her mare. Dale did the same with his roan. Laurie came hurrying after him, her auburn hair shining blood-dark in the moonlight. Glencannon saw that she carried the .44 Remington he'd given her hanging limp in one hand; he reached out and took it from her.

"Jim," she said, and there was some of the same relief and tenderness in the way she spoke his name as in the way she'd spoken Dale's. "Jim, what happened?"

"Dollar Wagon was camped a couple miles back," Glencannon told her quickly. "Soon as Halacy and his men were asleep, this fool kid showed up. Hiding in the trees for some while, I reckon, just waiting to get himself killed."

"I wouldn't have gotten killed," Dale said. He still sounded confused, as if he couldn't make up his mind whether to be angry, grateful, stubborn, or afraid. "I was going to take Halacy away from there at gunpoint and make him admit he killed pa."

"Sure you were. You'd never have left that camp alive, boy."

Laurie said, "How did you get him away, Jim?"

"He can tell you that later. There's no time now."

"He can tell me? Why not you?"

"Because I'm riding back for the Dollar Wagon," Glencannon said.

Her face showed alarm. "But why?"

"Chances are they left it alone when they took out after us. Or maybe posted one man to guard it. I figure there might be evidence inside that'll clear me of killing that tow-headed shill in Wild

154

Horse. If I'm right and I deliver the wagon to Sheriff Oldham, he'll have to believe the truth about Halacy."

"I'll go with you," Dale said, "I'll —"

"You won't do anything," Glencannon told him gruffly. "You've done enough already." He squinted down at the holster strapped on the youth's belt, realizing that it was empty. "What happened to that cap-and-ball of yours?"

Dale looked down at his scuffed boots. "I . . . I lost it in the trees after you started shooting."

"Damn." Glencannon jerked the .44-40 Winchester out of his saddle scabbard, handed it to Laurie. "You take this. The handgun'll do me better now anyway."

"What do you want us to do?"

"Hide in the rocks where you can watch this road and the main one down below. Keep the horses out of sight and quiet. Even if Halacy and his bunch come up here, they won't find you; you'll be all right until morning. Then head straight back for the ranch. I'll see you there."

Laurie hesitated briefly, as if she wanted to say something, or maybe embrace him as she had earlier. But then she nodded, caught hold of Dale's arm, and prodded him into taking the roan and her mare farther away into the rocks.

Glencannon went on foot to where he could look back down the slope to the east. Halacy and what looked to be two other riders were visible on the main road, riding more slowly, trailing columns of dust. They could see now that there

155

was no longer any dust in front of them and Halacy would know that his quarry had left the road. But he wouldn't know if they had hidden somewhere along the river, crossed the river, or taken to the badlands. Rage and frustration would keep them out and searching the area for a time, if Glencannon was any judge of a son of a bitch like Halacy, and that was all the time he would need to make his assault on the Dollar Wagon.

He hurried back down to where the sorrel waited. Laurie had come back there too, and when he reached her she said, "Jim . . . be careful. I've got Dale back now; I don't want to lose you instead."

He let those words pass without dwelling on their meaning, just as he had with the other things she had said to him on this day, and the kisses she had let him have. This was not the time; later perhaps, but not now. "You'd best get out of sight," he said. "They're not far away now and they might take a notion to come up this way any time."

"All right. But you will be careful?"

"I will. Don't worry about me, Laurie; just take care of yourself and Dale."

He swung into the saddle, heeled the sorrel around and took it to the north along this side of the rise. The ground here was rocky and made for slow going, but the hillock ran for a quarter mile or so in irregular formation and formed a protective barrier between him and the main road where Halacy was. He rode as fast as he dared, mostly letting the tired sorrel pick its own way among the rocks and around berry bushes and scrub trees. When the hillock ended and he emerged onto open ground he paused alongside an overhang to look back to the south. He could still see dust down there, and none nearer where he was: they hadn't turned back yet. He'd judged Halacy correctly. Now he could concentrate on getting past the guard — three riders meant that the fourth had been posted back at the camp — and into the Dollar Wagon.

He rode down across dry grassland, through a narrow stand on juniper, and back onto the Wild Horse road. Ten minutes after that he reached the incline that led up onto the bluff. And at the end of another five minutes he had tied the sorrel to that same dead cedar log and was belly-down on that patch of grass near the cutaway, looking downslope at the Dollar Wagon.

He didn't see the guard at first. All he saw was the wagon, and that the dappled gray, still out of harness, was the only horse left in camp. The fire had been put out, but there was enough moonlight to make most of the clearing visible.

The brief flare of a match showed him where the guard was: on the far side of the wagon near the tailgate, probably facing toward the secondary track and the trees that flanked it. Glencannon nodded to himself in the darkness, slid a hand down to the still unfamiliar Remington in

157

his holster and made sure it was jammed tight into the leather. Then he eased forward over the edge and began to make his way down the slope.

Thorns from the gooseberry bushes scratched his hands and face, but Glencannon took no notice. His eyes were watchful, his mouth set in hard lines, and he made sure each step was silent. It took him at least ten minutes to reach the bottom without dislodging any loose rocks or alerting the hidden guard. Another match had flared when he was halfway down — either the man over there was nervous or he liked his tobacco — and now, as he crouched behind one of the bushes at the edge of the clearing, the glow butt end of a cigarette arced out into the darkness beyond the wagon.

Glencannon drew the Remington, held it loosely in his hand as he started to raise up from behind the bush. But in that same instant something made a clattering noise on the bluff that rose up across the river.

The guard came out from behind the wagon almost immediately, a handgun upraised in one hand. Glencannon thought it might be the one called Luke. He hunkered down again and stayed motionless, letting the shadows hide him. But the other man's attention was on the opposite bluff, and after a moment he started cautiously in that direction. There were no more sounds. The first ones, Glencannon thought, had been made by some nocturnal animal come to nibble berries or drink from the river. He waited, watching as the man moved closer to the riverbank.

When Luke's back was to him Glencannon eased up and began to catwalk toward the wagon. Partway there, while he was still in the open, the other man stopped and half-turned; but he hadn't heard anything behind him and he didn't come all the way around. Glencannon kept moving, up on the toes of his boots, and finally reached the shadows along the wagon's near side, where his rifle bullets had pocked the gaudy paint earlier. He laid his back against the wood, put his head out just far enough so he could keep Luke in sight.

It took the man another three minutes to decide that there was no danger anywhere near the river. Then he came back toward the wagon, still holding the gun but pointed down at the ground at his side. With his free hand he fished into his shirt pocket for the makings, drew them out. It was clear from the angle at which he was moving that he intended to take up his former position on the far side of the wagon. Glencannon, watching, reversed the .44 in his hand. His own intention was to wait until the man was settled again, then creep around and lay the Remington's butt end alongside his skull.

But that wasn't what happened. Luke was some less than ten paces from the wagon when some animal instinct warned him; he stopped, stood frozen with the gun half up in one hand and the makings clenched in the other. Glencannon, on the same kind of instinct, tried to pull back tighter against the wagon. But when he did that he shuffled his feet and his bootheel clumped against one of the wheel spokes, making an audible noise.

Luke took two running steps to his left, dropping the sack of Bull Durham, and cut loose with two quick shots. Glencannon had already thrown himself away from the wagon and flat on the ground; neither of the bullets hit him as he rolled, pain lashing in his wounded shoulder, trying to get the .44 reversed back again. The other man fired a third time as Glencannon rolled onto his knees. That slug ripped along his shirtfront, opening the fabric but not breaking the skin. Reflex made him pitch and roll again. Another bullet came so close to his head that it sprayed bits of dirt into his face, blinding him momentarily. He got his finger on the trigger of the .44, came back up on his knees, and returned the fire even though he couldn't see where he was shooting.

He heard a strange mixture of sounds as he pawed at his dirt-stung eyes: the ricocheting chink of metal against metal, another whistling shot, a matter which made him think the guard had lost his gun, and a savage yell that seemed to confirm it. His vision came back blurrily. He hadn't dropped the man, he saw then, or even winged him; one of his shots had struck the handgun, kicked it loose and thrown it away somewhere in the darkness. But Luke wasn't through yet: he came hurtling forward, yelling like an Indian, and in his hand now Glencannon caught the glint and wicked shape of a Bowie knife.

A Bowie was one of the most deadly of hand weapons, horn-handled, with a curved, single-edged, foot-long blade, and Glencannon had seen what it could do to a man in close quarters. Fear cut at him; he snapped a shot at the onrushing figure. But it was wild, and before he could squeeze off again the man lashed out with one boot and drove the heel against Glencannon's right forearm. The Remington popped loose from his fingers, spun away. And the Bowie knife flashed downward, shining evilly in the spill of moonlight.

Glencannon managed to duck away from the flashing blade, to kick out with his own leg against Luke's shin. The man was already off-balance from his lunge; he went down hard and half on top of Glencannon, taking away some of his breath, making him flop fishlike under the pinning weight. A heavy forearm jammed against his throat as Luke rolled over astride him. The knife went up again, straight above his right eye.

Desperately Glencannon twisted backward and jackknifed his legs perpendicular to the ground, locking his boots around the other man's head. Then he jerked forward, pitched the heavy weight off him to one side, and scrambled over onto all fours, up onto his feet — choking,

161

fighting for breath, his throat on fire from the brutal forearm thrust.

The other man had scuttled away too, had kicked the Remington out of reach. Now he began circling Glencannon, waving the Bowie, waiting for an opening. Glencannon tried to dance sideways toward the wagon a few feet away; the man thrust suddenly, narrowly missed Glencannon's ribcage as he twisted aside. But the thrust had put him off-balance again, and that was the opening Glencannon needed. He threw himself on the man coming in behind the knife, catching hold of the wrist. They both went down again, jarring into the hard earth, but this time it was Glencannon who landed on top.

Luke made an agonized grunting noise under him and his whole body went as stiff as a length of board lumber. Then, just as suddenly, the stiffness dissolved into a rag-doll laxity; Glencannon heard a small sigh much like that of a balloon losing air. He shoved off the man, gained his feet. A dark patch of liquid began to seep out from beneath the limp body at the spot where his right hand was pinned. Glencannon could see the bone handle of the Bowie knife; he couldn't see the blade but he knew where it was.

Twelve inches of that kind of honed steel could cut through a man's chest like a hot poker through a tub of butter.

Fourteen

Glencannon backed over to the Dollar Wagon and leaned against it, rubbing his throat and trying to get his breathing gentled down to normal again. His knees felt weak and shaky; any man who survived a fight with a Bowie knife could count himself lucky, and had better offer up a prayer to the Almighty that he never would have to take that challenge another time.

When he could breathe again without gasping he listened for the sounds of approaching riders. But there were none; the night was hushed, the secondary trail and the surrounding terrain was empty as they'd been before. He pushed away from the wagon, located and collected the Remington, and then dragged the dead man into the nearby bushes, out of sight. Back at the wagon, he hoisted himself onto the tailgate, wincing at the flash of pain in his shoulder. The wound was bleeding again — he could feel a thin wet trickle of blood along his back — but there was no time to worry about that now. Clenching his teeth, he untied the canvas flapback and moved inside.

By the light of a match he found a mill lantern and lit the wick. The wide interior was jammed with the wares he had seen displayed in Wild

Horse, as well as the monte layout, several trunks, grub sacks of flour and rice and dried fruit, cases of Doctor Modora's Tapeworm Remedy and Doctor Modora's Elixir and Vita-Tonic. Glencannon set the lantern on top of one of the wooden cases and began his search.

The first thing he found was a pair of breech-loading rifles and two boxes of ammunition for them. He made sure one of the rifles was loaded and set it aside. The trunks were stuffed with clothes, most of them fancy. One had a collection of women's garters and a pack of playing cards with obscene paintings on their backs; another yielded a yellowed newspaper clipping from a town in New Mexico that told of another Halacy — Jersey Jack's brother? — being hanged for horse thievery seven years earlier. But it was in a pair of cabinets along one side that he found what he was looking for.

There were eighteen packs of playing cards, all of them marked, and ten pairs of loaded dice for use with a roll of felt on which a craps layout had been printed. A sack in one cabinet contained half a dozen wallets, all of them of good quality and all containing the identification of men in Dakota and Wyoming settlements. Another sack was filled with gold rings, cufflinks, stickpins, expensive hunting-style watches; two of the watches had engravings that identified their owners. Six handguns hung in the second cabinet, one with intricate filigree work, another with a carved ivory grip; but the two most interesting by far were a plain Colt Peacemaker and a plain Dragoon Colt with a name scratched into the butt.

The Peacemaker belonged to him.

And the name on the Dragoon's butt was *Clay Brewer.*

Tight-lipped, Glencannon put the Dragoon back into the cabinet and secured the doors. He wanted things to be pretty much where he'd found them when he brought the Dollar Wagon into Wild Horse for Sheriff Oldham's inspection. But he checked to make sure the Peacemaker was loaded and then switched it for the Remington in his holster, tossing the unfamiliar weapon onto the grub-sacks. Then he turned back toward the rear, getting ready to leave.

He was reaching up for the lantern when he heard the oncoming pound of hoofbeats.

Quickly he caught up the lantern and snuffed the wick. When he peeled back an edge of the canvas flapback he could see a single rider come charging down the secondary trail, the tails of a frock coat fanned out behind him. In the downspill of moonlight he recognized the slick-haired monte dealer, Jess.

Glencannon already had the Peacemaker in his hand; he moved it up across his body and held it there, ready. Jess rode into the clearing but didn't draw rein until he'd angled toward the front of the wagon, out of Glencannon's line of sight. A moment later a shout went up.

"Luke? Hey, Luke, where are you?"

Glencannon made a loud grunting noise as though in answer.

"What in hell're you doin' in the wagon?" the dealer called. Glencannon heard him urge his horse back to the rear. "Shag ass, will you? We've got to move out right away. Jersey Jack's waitin' on us."

Glencannon grunted again. He still had his eye up to the slit between the flap and the wagon's side; he saw the horse's bobbing head come into view, then Jess's loose grip on the reins, and finally the dealer himself, bent forward in the saddle.

"Luke, damn you, come on out —"

With his left hand Glencannon whipped the flap aside, stepped through onto the tailgate. The Peacemaker was up in his hand as he snapped, "Hold it right there, mister."

But Jess didn't hold it. A mixture of surprise and fury flashed over his face and his right hand dove for the gun holstered at his side, while his left jerked the reins to bring the horse away from the wagon. Glencannon had no choice; he triggered the .44, felt its recoil the length of his arm. The horse reared, tossing its head wildly, forelegs pawing the air, and Jess went tumbling out of the saddle. He hit the ground on his buttocks and pitched over on one side, shouting with pain.

Glencannon couldn't be sure if his bullet had driven the man off or if he'd simply been thrown when the horse reared. He jumped down off the tailgate and approached the writhing figure cautiously, his weapon extended in front of him. Jess rolled over on his back, staring up with pain-clouded eyes. He was clutching his chest, high on the left side.

"You son of a bitch," he said, grimacing, "you busted my shoulder."

"If you make another move toward that gun of yours," Glencannon told him, "I'll bust the other one."

Jess ran his tongue over his lips. He had been belligerent the other two times Glencannon had seen him up close, but most of the toughness was gone now that he was hurt and under the gun. He said sullenly, "I'm not movin'."

"Where's Halacy?"

"I got nothin' to say to you."

"You've got plenty to say." Glencannon thumbed the hammer back on the Peacemaker. "And not much time to say it in."

"You . . . you wouldn't kill me," Jess said, but there was fear mixed with the pain in his eyes now.

"Try me, mister."

Jess read the expression on Glencannon's grim face. He rubbed the back of his good forearm across his mouth. "All right," he said. "All right, goddamn you."

"Where's Halacy?"

"Up in Gold Buttes."

"The ghost town?"

"Yeah."

"What's he doing there?"

Jess hesitated.

"Answer me. Why did Halacy go to Gold Buttes?"

"We winter up there sometimes. Got a place fixed up, extra stores —"

"You're holding back something," Glencannon said sharply. He aimed the .44's muzzle at Jess's left leg. "Spill it or I'll put a bullet in your knee cap and hobble you for life."

"All right! He took the woman and the kid there, him and Ben."

Glencannon went cold inside. "Woman and the kid?"

"That's right. We were huntin' for you up along the old trail and flushed them two instead —"

Glencannon dropped to one knee beside the dealer and gathered the man's shirtfront in his big hand, pulling the white face close to his. Jess howled in pain at the sudden wrenching.

"How did you flush 'em?" Glencannon demanded. "What happened?"

"Nothin' happened. Jesus, my shoulder —"

"Talk to me!"

Jess's adam's apple pumped up and down three times before he said, "We stopped to reconnoiter, that's all. Horse made a sound some ways off in he rocks and when we got over there we flushed the woman and the kid. Woman tried to throw down on us with a rifle but Halacy took it away from her. Then the kid got feisty, blurted out he knew Halacy'd killed his pa, and we had to cuff him around."

"You cuff the woman around too?" Glen-cannon asked in a deadly voice.

"No! Not while I was there, I swear to Christ! Halacy tied 'em both on their horses and him and Ben took 'em up to Gold Buttes. That's all I know, I swear to Christ . . ."

Glencannon cursed himself for a dauncehead and six kinds of a fool. He shouldn't have left Laurie and Dale up there alone; he should have stayed with them, or taken them with him when he backtrailed to the north. But how could he have guessed Halacy and his rannihans would ride that far up the Gold Buttes trail and Laurie's or Dale's horse would make a noise at just the wrong time? How could he have guessed?

He couldn't — except that that didn't make him any less of a fool or excuse his stupid damned carelessness. If anything happened to either Laurie or Dale . . .

Through his teeth he said to Jess, "So Halacy sent you back here to fetch the Dollar Wagon up to Gold Buttes."

"That's right, yeah."

"And then what?"

"I . . . I don't know."

Glencannon knew. If he was any judge of a bastard like Jersey Jack Halacy, the outlaw would want no one alive who might present a threat to him. He wouldn't hesitate to kill a woman or a boy. Or to rape a woman before he killed her, either.

"Which building would Halacy put the woman and the boy in?" he snapped.

"Reckon the old general store. That's the place Sid keeps fixed up for us."

"Who's Sid?"

"Old timer who lives up there year-round. Tetched and mean, but he likes Jack and does for him."

"Anybody else up there?"

"No." Jess coughed; blood dribbled out of the corner of his mouth. "Nobody else."

Glencannon released the man's shirt; Jess sank back on the hard ground, moaning softly, his fingers kneading the blood-soaked area where the Peacemaker's lead had taken him.

Standing, Glencannon tried to think. He had to get up to Gold Buttes before Halacy and the other two turned loose on Laurie and decided to finish both her and the boy. But how? If he remembered right, only that one rutted wagon road led up into the ghost town — it was walled by steep shale bluffs on two sides, by a deep sheersided canyon on a third — and Halacy figured to have that road watched. Damn it, he couldn't just ride in —

Or could he?

An idea formed in Glencannon's mind. He knelt once again beside the dealer. Jess had passed out from shock and pain; he lay breathing thickly through his nose, blood still dribbling from one corner of his mouth. Quickly Glencannon stripped off the frock coat and the fancy britches, then shed his own Levi's and put on the britches and the coat. They were a snug fit, but he found that he could move freely enough.

He went back inside the wagon, found some rope and a blanket, and took them back to where Jess lay. He bound the dealer's hands and feet, covered him with the blanket. Then he set about harnessing the dappled gray to the Dollar Wagon.

Ten minutes later Glencannon was up on the wagon's high seat, the gray's reins clenched tight in one hand. He brought the gray around and up onto the secondary trail. When he reached the main road he urged the animal forward at full speed, but before long the lurching, bone-jarring jolt of the wagon on the rough roadbed forced him to slow down. He kept the gray at a steady, even pace, though every fiber of him cried out for speed and his muscles and nerves were stretched wire-taut.

He couldn't risk a broken axle, or a possible weakening of the undercarriage, especially on that badly rutted Gold Buttes road. In the darkness, even with the moonlight, it was possible he could pass for the dealer; and if so he had a chance of getting into Gold Buttes alive, of rescuing Laurie and Dale. But he couldn't do either of those thing if he failed to keep the Dollar Wagon and himself in one piece.

Like it or not, this was one race against time he *had* to ride slow and careful.

Fifteen

It took him forty minutes to reach the turnoff from the main road, and another twenty after that to raise the fork that led up to the ghost town. When he passed the place where he'd left Laurie and Dale in hiding, anguish sliced through him and he could feel his heart slugging in his chest.

There was no use in lying to himself any longer. He cared for Laurie, cared for her deeply; always had, from that first day he'd met her when he was some less than Dale's age. And she cared for him, too, and always had. Her words to him back at the ranch and on the long hot ride across the badlands made that plain enough. She'd been Clay's wife, yes, but Clay hadn't been her husband for more than a year and now Clay was dead. She deserved some happiness after all the pain she had suffered — and he'd treated her coldly, or worse, like a wanton. Maybe she deserved better than Jim Glencannon, but if he was what she wanted, then she'd have him. And gladly, for his part. Gladly.

No more lying at all now: he loved that woman, and he'd tell her so first chance he had.

He'd get into Gold Buttes and take her and

Dale safely away from Halacy — he *had* to. By God, no matter what it took, he had to!

He reined the gray onto the left fork, shouting "Heeyaw, Heeyaw!" to keep it plunging ahead. The wheels clattering along the deep ruts made the wagon shake like a dog after a bath; Glencannon gritted his teeth, as he had had to do before, against the bite of pain in his shoulder. The wound had opened up again and bled off and on; the back of his shirt was plastered tight against his skin. He could feel the arm stiffening up as it had yesterday, kept flexing his fingers to maintain circulation. He'd be able to use it when the time came, he was sure of that in the same way he was sure he would find Laurie and Dale unharmed. But even if he had to face down Halacy as a one-armed cripple, he'd manage it somehow.

At one time, probably at the height of Gold Buttes' boom, somebody had nailed a sign to a stunted cottonwood a short ways beyond the apex of the fork. In the moonlight Glencannon could read it as he passed: *Welcome to Gold Buttes — The City of Gold Opportunity*. The sign hung in two rotting pieces now, swaying slightly in the faint night breeze, its paint weather-faded, like an epitaph in a graveyard.

The road wound upward through boulders and rock-strewn clearings, past stands of spruce and juniper. It's surface was less rutted here, where the ground was mostly dust-covered rock, and the bucking of the wagon slackened as its thoroughbraces absorbed the shock. The gray wheezed audibly as it labored over the steep terrain, pitching its head from side to side; but it never balked and Glencannon had no need for the whip slotted by his right leg.

He looked out and along his backtrail once, after a few minutes had crawled away, but the looming trees and high craggy outcroppings had long since sealed off any view of the river or of the badlands trail. The rest of the time he kept his eyes on the road ahead. But thus far, there was nothing to see there either. Everything had a frozen, whitish look in the moonlight, as if the rocks and trees had been dusted with talcum. Nothing moved anywhere; the only sounds were the clatter of the wheels, the snorting of the gray, his own tense breathing.

But the stillness and the frozen beauty were deceptive; Glencannon knew that as well as any man. These badlands were anything but tame. They harbored a dozen different kinds of predators, presented a hundred different threats to a man's life, offered a thousand different hardships. This was wild country. It had been for eons and it would always be.

During the Gold Rush days, when extremes were the ordinary way of life, it had been at its wildest. Men had come here then for the first time in numbers; Indians had been pushed here, Custer had died here, and settlers who had lived for gold and ended up instead with a few acres of hardscrabble land nearby. The hills had been latticed with tunnels, flumes, and hydraulic monitors. Miners had paid a dollar for a beef-steak and another dollar for the plate to eat it from. Towns like Gold Buttes had blossomed and wilted like quick-blooming desert cactus. And a great many men had died, in accidents and from snakebite and in gunfights and at the hands of murderers and thieves like Jersey Jack Halacy.

Before this night was through, Glencannon thought grimly, still more men would die in the wilderness of Gold Buttes.

The road ran along the shale cliffs which bordered the town, and for a time Glencannon had trouble holding the wagon on the landslid road. When he looked down the sheer sides of the canyon on his left he couldn't see the bottom in the dense shadows. Sweat caked him and his muscles were corded with tension when he finally neared the one final curve before the trail entered the wide box which held the town.

As he neared the curve he could see the silhouette of the headframe of Consolidated Mining Union's shaft towers, looming against the moonlit sky. He brought the gray up a dozen rods from the bend, sat listening and scanning the rock wall above, trying to catch some indication of a posted guard. But he neither saw nor heard anything.

He started the gray again. Entering the bend, he kept his head low, his back bent into a slouch and Jess's hat pulled down over his eyes. He had the wagon halfway through the turn when the guard showed himself.

The man had been hidden in the darkness high on the bluff, behind a ledge-balanced boulder. Glencannon thought that if he'd tried to hunt him without knowing his exact location, he would never have found him without being seen first. The guard waved, leaning against the side off the boulder; Glencannon waved back. Not a word was spoken between them.

He took the gray through the curve, around a tall sharp spire and a short ways beyond. Then he stopped it again. For the first time he could see the moonlit outline of the abandoned town. It looked like what it was: a silent ghost. Gold Buttes had been a hell-raising town by reputation, and legend had it that there had been a stretch of five months when there was a murder committed every Saturday night. But now that it was dead, it seemed to draw in sound, as if in atonement for all the violence it had poured forth when alive.

It had also been a rich town in its heyday, financed by a large Eastern bank until the bedrock vein had been worked dry, and many of the buildings had been built to last. It had produced over fifteen million dollars in gold in its short life span, Glencannon knew, and at the beginning, before the surface placers ran out, it had not been uncommon for miners to take out $1,000 a day. Then the Eastern bank had put in the shafts and milked it dry; beyond the town Glencannon could see the black forest of what was left of Consolidated Mining Union's holdings.

He spent a minute reorienting himself with the town proper. One of the buildings showed flickering light through cracks in its boarding and sealed-up windows; that would be "Moran Bros. Cheap Cash Store," the old general store Jess had told him about. Tied at the crumbling hitch rail in front were four horses. Glencannon couldn't be sure at the distance, but he thought one was Laurie's shaggy-rumped mare and the other Dale's roan.

He climbed down, moved to the rear, and lifted himself onto the tailgate. Before he could go in after Laurie and Dale, he had to eliminate the threat of the guard — escape would be impossible otherwise — and he had to do it quickly and quietly. Gunshots or any warning yell would alert Halacy and the other man that something was wrong.

Inside the wagon he found another coil of rope, looped it over his good shoulder. On the roadbed again he hurried downtrail around the tall sharp spire, keeping his head bent so that the hat shielded his face. When he reached the vicinity of the guard's hiding place on the bluff's side he pulled up and began making an agitated beckoning gesture with his right arm.

At first there was no sign of movement from the irregular black shape of the boulder. Glencannon kept waving his arms, his head still lowered to keep his face in shadow. Finally the dark figure of the guard rose up. The man stood motionless for a moment, then began to make his way down the steep slope to the road, his rifle held loosely at his side. When he reached the trail Glencannon could see that he was a grizzled, wild-bearded man in his sixties, the one the monte dealer had called Sid. He shambled toward Glencannon, the moonlight showing a puzzled expression on his seamed features.

"What's the matter, Jess?" he called as he approached. "Hell's fire, you —"

Glencannon didn't let him finish the sentence. He pivoted and jumped forward, swung his balled right hand in a sweeping arc. His knuckles exploded on the point of Sid's chin, almost lifting the older man off his feet as it sent him sprawling backward. Glencannon was on him immediately, but there was no need for further violence; Sid was unconscious and looked as if he would stay that way for some time.

With the rope from the Dollar Wagon, Glencannon tied the man's arms and legs securely, and then used Sid's own bandana for a gag. He picked up the rifle, emptied the magazine into the canyon, and carried the weapon with him back to the wagon. He stowed it under the seat.

He paused then, rubbing his scraped knuckles, pondering his next move. As far as he could see, he had two alternatives: he could drive the wagon straight into town, bring it up in front of Moran Bros. Cheap Cash Store, and hope its arrival would bring Halacy and the one called Ben outside where he could get the drop on them; or he could go in on foot, keeping to cover and shadow until he reached the general store, and hope to surprise them that way.

He discarded the latter choice as the riskier of the two. For one thing, Halacy might have heard the Dollar Wagon's approach and be looking for it; if it failed to come, the fact would make him suspicious. For a second thing, Glencannon wanted those two clear of Laurie and Dale if and when the shooting started, and it would be more difficult to accomplish that if he proceeded on foot. And for a third thing, he couldn't chance being seen or heard before he got to the store. Halacy was liable to harm one or both of his hostages without hesitation if he thought he was being stalked.

No, Glencannon thought, his one hope lay in continuing his masquerade, seeing it all the way through to the end, the same way you had to see through a bluff in a high-pot poker game. And he thought he knew a way now to guarantee that the arrival of the Dollar Wagon would bring Halacy and Ben out of Moran's. Bring them out in a hurry, too, and with luck, off their guard.

Glencannon climbed back onto the seat, took hold of the reins, clucked the gray into a walk. The road passed the rim of the canyon, widening somewhat as it became the main street of Gold Buttes. Tall grass grew in random patches on its surface, and there were tumbleweeds and tangles of brush and debris which had been pushed by the wind against the high curbs of the board sidewalks.

The first of the decaying buildings that lined both sides of the streets was a saloon, all of its windows either removed by the last of the former residents or broken by wind and storm. Next to it was the Adams Express Building, made of rhyolite tuff, a material common to the area; and then the small, frame butcher shop that had once had a floor made of Italian marble. Opposite was Mitch's Hotel, owned and operated by a three-hundred-pound woman named Mitch until she had been caught in a compromising situation by her husband and then shot.

Glencannon, sitting slouched but tight-drawn, his eyes restless and wary under the hatbrim, passed each of these structures in turn, keeping the gray's pace steady but rapid. He also passed the Hotel Bar, the Old French laundry that had been run by a Chinese from California, and a small dry-goods store with its front door hanging oddly by a single hinge. There was no sound anywhere save for the clatter of the wagon's wheels on the rough street, the faint soughing of a thin dry breeze blowing down from the high cliffs beyond the town.

On the next corner was the tallest of Gold Buttes' buildings, the Odd Fellows-Masonic Hall; it stood atilt now, its pointed roof collapsed into the third story. When Glencannon neared it he lifted the Colt Peacemaker onto his lap with his right hand, holding the reins with his stiffening left. The general store was in the next block, the town's last. From street level, more lamplight seemed to spill out through its rotting walls than he'd seen from above. It made the buildings look like an island in the sea of moon-etched darkness that surrounded it.

He used the reins to pick up the gray's speed then, the inside of his mouth dry with tension, the muscles in his legs and arms wiredrawn. And when the animal was running he slid the Peacemaker into his left hand, hauled up the whip from its slot near the brake, and snapped it sharply over the horse's head. The gray broke stride at first, but when he used the whip twice more it lowered its head in fright and ran full out.

Glencannon cracked the whip another time, then let it fail on the seat beside him and caught hold of the Peacemaker again. He leaned his body forward as they reached past the Miner's Cafe, a mercantile shop, the remaining three walls of Jon's Apothecary, pretending to jerk back on the reins, as if fighting the gray. And at the top of his voice he set up a yell.

"Runaway! Help me out here! Runaway horse!"

They were coming on Moran's store now. The gray's plunging head was within ten rods of it when the front door flew open, letting an amber elongation of lantern light spill over the cracked boarding of the sidewalk in front, and two men rushed out. Glencannon hauled back on the reins, bringing the gray up a little as they clattered on past toward the assayer's office next door. Then he stood up on the swaying floorboards and lept out to the side.

He landed on his feet, stumbled, went down. He hit the rough surface of the street on his left shoulder, causing fiery pain to erupt in his wound, then rolled and came up on his knees. He had kept a firm grip on the Peacemaker; he raised it in his hand, finger tightening on the trigger.

The two men had come into the street past the tied horses and were running toward him. They'd thought at first, just as he'd counted they would, that he was Jess; neither of them had his handgun drawn. But when they saw him come up with the Peacemaker they recognized him. Halacy shouted, "It's Glencannon!" and both he and the one named Ben pulled up and went for leather.

Ben got his gun out first, triggered a wild shot that plowed up sod thirty feet to Glencannon's left. Glencannon had him sighted; he squeezed off, saw dust puff out and blood appear on the man's shirtfront. Ben whirled half around, lost his gun, and sprawled face down in the street.

The horses were rearing at the hitch rail, pulling at their lines; the roan and one of the others broke loose first and went charging away upstreet in panic. Glencannon fired at Halacy at the same time the outlaw threw lead at him, but neither of them came close to hitting the other because of the plunging and scrambling horses. As the mare and the fourth horse broke their lines and ran after the other two, Glencannon threw himself flat, rolled, came up on belly and forearms this time. Halacy had hesitated for an instant, as if undecided whether to try for the general store's bright light some distance away or make for shadowed cover nearby. He chose the latter and was already moving toward a rough-hewn horse trough in front of the assayer's office.

Glencannon snapped a shot at him, missed; Halacy dove headlong behind the trough. Realizing what a perfect target he made himself, Glencannon shoved onto his feet and ran for the opposite side of the street and the darkness alongside another of Gold Buttes' saloons.

Two shots chased him there but neither bullet hit him. He leaned back against the building's wall, dragging breath into his lungs, peering across the street. A standoff, he thought bitterly. Both he and Halacy needed to reach the general store, and Laurie and Dale, to win this battle. If Halacy could regain his hostages, he could force Glencannon to throw down his weapon and surrender. Getting to them would be uppermost in his mind, just as it was uppermost in Glencannon's.

Yet the way things stood now, neither of them could reach the front of Moran's and pass through that lanternlit doorway without taking a bullet from the other. Glencannon was already thinking of other ways to get inside, and to avoid Halacy and prevent him from getting in as well; he knew that Halacy, behind the trough over there, had to be doing the same.

This was going to be a dark and deadly game of cat-and-mouse, played among the ruined ghosts of Gold Buttes. Both men knew it and both had to accept it. The only questions now were who would make the first move and who would make the last.

The waiting began.

Sixteen

Neither man made a move for almost five minutes.

It was cooler up here than it had been down by the river, with the faint dry breeze blowing at this higher elevation, but Glencannon was soaked with sweat and a feverish, brassy dryness coated his mouth and clogged his throat. He had to keep ducking his head against his stiff left arm to clear the dripping wetness from his eyes.

Finally, to see if he would draw fire, he poked his head out of the shadows. Halacy gave him fire, all right: three quick shots, one of which sent splinters flying from the siding near Glencannon's shoulder. He jerked back, flattening himself against the wall again. But as soon as he did that, Halacy levered up from behind the trough and ran in a zig-zagging crouch into the narrow walkspace between Moran's and the assayer's office. Glencannon threw lead after him, missing wide both times. Halacy disappeared into the darkness.

Glencannon's teeth came together in a tight-jawed grimace. Now Halacy had the advantage; if that walkspace went all the way through to the rear, he could move straight back and then around into the general store by the rear entrance. Halacy might also be crouched there in the shadows, waiting for Glencannon to show himself again, but that was a chance Glencannon had to take. If he waited here too long, and Halacy got inside the store, it might cost Laurie and Dale their lives.

He steadied himself, then dodged out of the shadows and ran along the boardwalk in front of the saloon. Halacy was still waiting across the street; two wild shots followed him as he plunged around the far corner and into the alleyway between the saloon and the old jail. He dropped to one knee in the protective darkness, sleeving sweat off his forehead and out of his eyes. Listening, he heard nothing but silence from across the street. Had Halacy picked up and headed back through the walkspace this time? Or was he still waiting at the front corner?

Glencannon came up into a crouch, took two quick sidling steps out of the alley. This time, coming into the open, he didn't draw fire. He took two more steps, still didn't draw it, and kept on going in a low-bent dash across the street. His angle was toward the lighted rectangle of Moran's front door; if Halacy had gone around to the back, he could go straight in through that front entrance . . .

But Halacy hadn't gone around to the back. There was a muzzle flash from the walkspace, the sudden echoing roar of a shot; a bullet sliced past so close that Glencannon could hear the hum of it in his left ear. He veered sharply away

186

from the outspill of light, over toward the alleyway on the opposite side of Moran's, and that movement saved his life: another slug missed him by inches, would have cut him down if he'd kept going straight ahead. He was almost to the boardwalk by then, where this section of it ended at the alley entrance. At the crack of a third shot he threw himself forward like a man diving off a rock into a swimming hole, landed skidding through a gather of tumbleweeds and rotting garbage. That bullet missed him too and he was able to scramble belly-down beyond the high curb, into the alley mouth. He kept on scrambling until he reached the store's side wall, then picked himself up and stood panting in the shadows near the corner.

He eased his head around for one quick look before jerking it back again. But the boardwalk in front of the store remained empty and there was no sign of Halacy at the far corner. He listened, ears keening the night like an animal's. He thought he heard a sound somewhere along the wall on the other side, but he couldn't be sure. If that walkspace went all the way through, would Halacy head back there now? He hadn't done that the first two times, but he might have been playing his own brand of cat-and-mouse. And he'd also had to reload; he'd thrown too much lead so far with that one handgun.

Damn it, *did* that walkspace go all the way through? He couldn't remember. If it did, and Halacy was heading back there, his own move was to duck around and go in through the front. But if Halacy was still waiting at the front corner, Glencannon would be a dead man the instant he stepped up onto the boardwalk . . .

He took another quick look across the front of the building. Still deserted. And his ears told him nothing either. He pawed away more sweat, and when he did that he noticed the dark shape of the building on the other side of the alley. It was two-storied and the ground floor had once belonged to the barber shop; but the upstairs had private rooms where some of the town whores had conducted their business. A low balcony ran along the front, shadowing the sidewalk beneath, and also along the side wall to the end of the alley. Most of its fancy gingerbread trim had been torn away and the supporting timbers looked to be termite-ridden. But the beams were reachable from the alley floor, and just might be sturdy enough even now to hold a man's weight.

If he could get up there, Glencannon thought, he'd have a better vantage point. He could cover both the front and back of Moran's that way, find out more easily where Halacy was and either pick him off or make his move for the store in an opposite direction. It was a gamble, but anything he did now was a gamble. And he had to do something; he couldn't just keep on standing here in the darkness, waiting for Halacy to come to him.

He listened again, heard nothing but the whispering rustle of the wind, and eased his Peacemaker into its holster. Wiping his hands on the

188

monte dealer's britches, he crossed the alley and judged the leap. Then he drew a breath, crouched and jumped. His fingers curled around the support beam, and he thought in that instant that if he made any kind of noise, if the nails and locust pegs began to pull loose, he'd have to drop off and try something else; he couldn't afford to have Halacy suspect where he was or what he was doing. But the beam held, and so did the remaining strength in his stiffened left arm. He swayed noiselessly for a moment, then managed to catch the toe of his boot in a crack between two of the wall boards. Using the crack as a step, he levered up and hauled himself onto the balcony.

Quickly he twisted around onto his knees, digging for his Colt, and crawled to where he could look along the front of Moran's. The boardwalk was empty, the front door still hanging open and lamplit. Nothing moved in the shadows in the walkspace beyond.

Glencannon waited, listening to the heavy thud of his heart. Then he crawled back the other way, along the side wall, the rotting timber under him making little groans of protest at his weight. But they were small sounds; he didn't think they would carry far.

When he was within a few rods of the rear corner he heard another sound, this one from behind the general store. He froze. The sound wasn't repeated, but a few seconds later he saw movement among the shadows at the back corner. He lifted the Peacemaker, sighting along the length of his arm.

The dark figure of Halacy appeared at the corner, peered around it up the alley.

The outlaw made a clear target, but just as Glencannon was about to squeeze off he shifted his weight slightly and one of the boards under him creaked again. Halacy's head jerked up. Glencannon fired, missed as Halacy ducked back behind the corner. No more than five seconds passed, and then there was the crash of a boot against wood and the squealing protest of hinges, and Glencannon suddenly realized that he might have outsmarted himself.

As long as he'd been on the ground, Halacy hadn't wanted to chance going through the back door of Moran's because it had been locked. Laurie and Dale were probably in the main part of the store, up front where the lantern was, and by the time Halacy could kick the door in and come through the store, Glencannon would have been alerted and would have gone in through the front. But with Glencannon up here on the balcony, Halacy must have figured he had enough time.

Glencannon knew he couldn't stop Halacy before the outlaw got inside. Cursing, he ran back along the balcony half a dozen strides and then launched himself off into the air. He had learned how to fall during a long summer of breaking horses up in Wyoming when he was younger; he let his body go slack, pulled his knees up slightly and threw his arms out wide. He landed on the balls of his feet, went over in a tight roll, and came back up on his feet again in the middle of the alley. He ran for the front corner, around it and up onto the boardwalk and into the open front doorway of Moran's.

He went in crouching low, moving diagonally toward the left-hand wall. The interior had been fixed up like a crude cabin, with tables and chairs and bunk beds; Laurie and Dale were trussed up and gagged in two of the bunks. But the long store counter was still there, on the far side of the room where the lighted lantern was, and Halacy was just coming up behind it from the rear. His mouth fell open in surprise when he saw Glencannon; he hadn't expected him to get in here that quickly. He pulled up and flung himself to one side, sending a barrel and the remains of somebody's supper toppling across the floor.

Glencannon snapped a shot that chipped wood from an empty shelf above Halacy's head. Halacy raised up behind the counter and returned the fire, but by then Glencannon had upended one of the tables and taken cover behind it, away from Laurie and Dale to keep them out of the line of fire. Bullets thwacked into the table, burying themselves in the heavy wood. Glencannon leaned around, threw another shot that scraped along the top of the counter. Then it was Halacy's turn, but this time he didn't fire at where Glencannon was.

He fired at the lantern.

The store room went dark for an instant, only to explode into blazing firelight. Kerosene from the lantern's shattered fount sprayed over the counter, carrying flames with it. The dry rotting wood began to burn like a bonfire, raising a sheet of flame between Halacy and Glencannon.

Through it, Glencannon saw the outlaw jump up and race back into the rear of the store. He fired after him, but the fire and the smoke obscured the running figure and he knew he'd missed. The flames were already beginning to spread, licking at the walls, sweeping across the floor; clouds of acrid woodsmoke poured through the room.

Glencannon shoved up and ran to where Laurie and Dale lay bound. Swiftly he tore at the knots in the ropes, wishing he had his Barlow knife that was back with the rest of his belongings in Wild Horse, knowing he had precious little time. He finally managed to loosen the ones around Laurie's wrists; he wrenched them off. The smoke was making her retch behind the filthy gag in her mouth, and he pulled that free too, then did the same for Dale. Next he set to work untying the boy's hands.

Coughing violently, Laurie stripped the ropes off her ankles and stumbled off the bunk. "Oh, Jim," she gasped, "thank God you're here! They were going to kill us, they were —"

"There's no time for that now," he told her. "Save your breath, don't talk."

He got Dale's hands loose, helped the youth

untie his feet, and hoisted him up onto his feet. The fire was still spreading, climbing the walls now; the whole rear section of the store was a dancing wall of flame. Glencannon crowded Laurie and Dale toward the front, but off to one side of the open doorway. Dale started toward the door, but Glencannon caught his arm and held him back.

"This whole place will go up any minute!" the boy yelled over the roar crackle of the fire. "We've got to get out of here!"

"No, not yet!"

Glencannon's every instinct told him that if they simply walked out that door there would be three bullets waiting for them the instant they hit the boardwalk. Halacy was ruthless and cunning, and he wouldn't leave Gold Buttes without first making sure that the three people who could send him to the gallows were dead. He'd have doubled around the side of Moran's, knowing that they couldn't leave through the rear because of the fire, and be waiting on one side or the other out front.

But which side?

Glencannon slid fresh cartridges from his belt, chambered them into the Peacemaker. He would have to go out first, alone; that much he knew for certain. But when he did he'd have to be looking one way or the other, and if he made the wrong choice of sides, he was liable to die for his mistake. And if he died, so would Laurie and Dale.

The smothering billows of smoke were thicker now and the fire had crept across the floor toward them. The heat seared Glencannon's face, threatened all of their clothing. Hurriedly he bit off instructions, telling them to wait until he was outside and there was no more shooting before they tried to come out. A protest from Laurie died in a spasm of coughing. Dale only nodded, put a protective hand on his mother's arm.

Glencannon pawed his eyes clear, took a half-step toward the center of the room, and then ran for the open doorway.

As soon as one boot cleared the threshold, he left his feet to twist his body sideways, facing south toward that side of Moran's where the barbershop was. He hit the rough planking of the sidewalk on his right shoulder, rolled off the high curb into the street. Two shots erupted from the direction he was looking: he had guessed correctly. One bullet tore the heel off his right boot, the second splintered wood from the planking. He rolled again, under the hitch rail, and brought his .44 up just as Halacy fired again.

Glencannon felt the bullet pass close along his right cheek. Through eyes that still watered badly from the smoke, he saw Halacy standing spread-legged at the corner of the building, lips skinned back, gun held straight out in front of him. Glencannon squeezed off twice, feeling the buck of the Peacemaker the length of his arm.

Halacy jerked upright, firing a fourth shot

wildly into the air, and then he spun in a half circle and fell into the pile of tumbleweeds and garbage at the end of the sidewalk.

Glencannon got painfully to his knees. Laurie and Dale rushed out of the burning store at once, ran to where he knelt in the street. Laurie knelt beside him, flinging her arm across his shoulders, hugging his face close to her breast.

"Jim!" she cried. "Jim, are you all right?"

He looked at her out of half-closed eyes. There were tears on her cheeks, but not the tears of fire and smoke; it was the first time he had ever seen her cry. "I reckon I'll live," he said gravely. "You and Dale?"

"We're fine — now. But we couldn't have stayed in there another second. If you —" She broke off, holding him, weeping.

Glencannon eased both her and himself upright. Dale was already standing above Halacy, peering down at the outlaw with clenched fists; Glencannon held Laurie away from him, went over next to the boy. When he turned Halacy he saw that his bullet had taken the man high on the right side of the chest. But Halacy wasn't dead, and Glencannon was grateful for that. He'd had enough of killing; the law would take care of Jersey Jack Halacy — the law and a gallows rope.

With Dale helping him, he pulled the unconscious outlaw into the street, away from the burning building. The fire had claimed all of Moran's now, and the flames from its blazing roof were already licking at the assayer's office and the barbershop-and-whorehouse. It wouldn't be long, Glencannon thought, before the whole block was aflame, and maybe the whole town. Might be best if that happened, instead of the town just rotting away or becoming a sanctuary for another outlaw band.

He gave his Peacemaker to Dale. "You watch over Halacy while I round up the horses and fetch the Dollar Wagon," he said.

When he had the boy's nod he moved away on bone-weary legs. Laurie came up beside him, put her arm around him again. And that was good, not only for the feel of her body against his but for the support she gave him. He didn't know how much longer he could hold out before exhaustion overtook him. Long enough to get clear of Gold Buttes, maybe, but not much longer.

It was going to be up to Dale and Laurie to get them out of the badlands and back to Wild Horse.

Seventeen

Sheriff Harrison Oldham was not a man who liked to eat crow. He stood at the foot of the bed, in the room at The Mason House where Glencannon was recuperating, and worried his hat with one hand and his droopy mustache with the other. His discomfort made Glencannon, propped against three soft feather pillows, feel even more comfortable than he had a minute ago.

"I just come from the jail," Oldham said gruffly. "Halacy still ain't talkin', but the one named Jess had plenty to say; he figures it might help save his neck. Said Halacy was the one who killed Clay Brewer and ordered the tow-head shot, so's to frame you. Along with what Miz Brewer told us and what was in the Dollar Wagon, I reckon that puts you in the clear."

Glencannon decided not to ruffle Oldham's feathers by saying anything smart-mouth; he might need the lawman for a friend someday. He said only, "Thanks, sheriff. Appreciate you stopping by."

"Yeah, well, figured I owed it to you. Not that I'm forgettin' the way you threw down on me and Riggins and them others, and made us chase you to hell and gone up in the Gold Buttes. I'll

197

be keepin' my eye on you as long as you're here in Wild Horse."

"That might be quite a while," Glencannon said.

"Oh? You fixin' on stayin' on here, are you?"

"I've been giving it some thought. You don't have any objections, do you?"

Oldham pondered for a moment. Then he shrugged and said, "Reckon I don't. Long as you stay out of trouble, that is."

"I plan on it, sheriff."

"Well, see that you do," Oldham said. He made a face, as if he'd tasted enough crow; then he turned on his heel and left the room.

Glencannon grinned after him. It was the day after he and Laurie and Dale had delivered the Dollar Wagon, with Halacy and the oldtimer named Sid trussed up inside, to the Wild Horse jail. He'd slept most of the way down out of the badlands, so that he was clear-headed when they arrived. As soon as Oldham had listened to his story, and to that of Laurie and Dale, he'd dispatched his deputy to bring Jess and the body of Luke in from the wagon's former camp-site; and he'd allowed Glencannon to come here to The Mason House under guard. Doctor Simpkins had come and dressed his shoulder wound, and then he'd slept again, this time for more than fifteen hours. He'd awakened only minutes before Oldham's arrival, feeling rested, if still stiff and sore and covered with bruises. In fact, he felt downright fine — better than he had in months, maybe years.

Then the door opened and Laurie entered the room, and he decided he felt better than he ever had in his life. She came over to the bed, looking fine and sweet in a calico dress with her auburn hair fluffed out over her shoulders, and sat beside him. He reached out, took her hand, held it tightly in his own big calloused one. There were no words between them and none needed. Her eyes told him everything he needed to know, and her lips confirmed it seconds later.

There would be no more fiddlefooted drifting for Jim Glencannon, no more lonely nights beside a string of long and lonely trails. He knew at last what it was he wanted, what he had always wanted deep down inside. And now that he had it, he was never going to let it go.

Laurie's hand would remain clasped in his for the rest of their days.

We hope you have enjoyed this Large Print book. Other G.K. Hall & Co. or Chivers Press Large Print books are available at your library or directly from the publishers.

For more information about current and up-coming titles, please call or write, without obligation, to:

G.K. Hall & Co.
295 Kennedy Memorial Drive
Waterville, ME 04901

Tel. (800) 223-1244
Tel. (800) 223-6121

OR

Chivers Press Limited
Windsor Bridge Road
Bath BA2 3AX
England
Tel. (0225) 335336

All our Large Print titles are designed for easy reading, and all our books are made to last.